Lurlene McDaniel

Last
DANCE

DARBY
CREEK
PUBLISHING

Cataloging-in-Publication

McDaniel, Lurlene.
[Will I ever dance again?]
Last dance / by Lurlene McDaniel.
        p. ; cm.
ISBN-13: 978-1-58196-031-0
ISBN-10: 1-58196-031-X
Summary: Rachel Deering, an otherwise normal 13-year-old aspiring
ballerina from Miami, suddenly finds herself in the hospital, diagnosed
with diabetes. Now she needs to learn how to manage her disease, and to
cope with being different from all her friends. Will she ever dance again?
1. Teenage girls—Juvenile fiction. 2. Diabetes—Juvenile fiction.
3. Ballet dancers—Juvenile fiction. 4. Friendship—Juvenile fiction.
[1. Teenage girls —Fiction. 2. Diabetes—Fiction. 3. Ballet dancers—
Fiction. 4. Friendship—Fiction.] I. Title. II. Author. III. Uniform title.
PZ7.M4784172 Las 2005
[Fic] dc22
OCLC: 60035873

Text copyright © 1982 by Lurlene McDaniel
Front cover photo by Photos.com/JupiterImages Corp. copyright © 2005
Back cover photo by iStockphoto copyright © 2005
Design by Kelly Rabideau

Published by Darby Creek Publishing
7858 Industrial Parkway
Plain City, OH 43064
www.darbycreekpublishing.com

Printed in the United States of America

OPM 4 6 8 10 9 7 5

978-1-58196-031-0

-ONE-

"**O**ne and two and stretch . . . and down. That's right! Up . . . up. Work with the inside of your leg. Yes . . . heel forward." The thick accent of Madame Pershoff's voice hung over the rehearsal hall like a cloud.

Rachel Deering rose high onto toe and then melted into a grand *plié*. She was very careful to keep her back straight and aligned. Was she tired! She couldn't remember a time when she felt less like being at ballet class.

"Come. Come, ladies!" Madame Pershoff scolded. "Straighten those backs. Hold those muscles!"

Easy for you to say, Rachel thought irritably. From her position at the barre, she could see the reflection of the white-haired woman sitting on her "throne"—a stiff-backed chair next to the pianist.

Rachel arched her arm over her head, and then bent to touch her forehead to her knee.

Oh, great! she thought. *I have to go to the bathroom—AGAIN!* But she didn't dare ask to be excused from barre work. *Why are ballet dancers expected to have iron bladders?* she asked herself.

Madame Pershoff tapped her silver-headed cane in time with the piano. It pounded on the sleek oak floors in perfect tempo. The sound echoed in Rachel's ears like a sledgehammer.

She reflected on what a rotten day it had been so far. Mr. Johnson had passed out a pop quiz in math (which she got only a 60 on). Mrs. Matthews had assigned more than fifty pages of history reading for the night. And Rachel had arrived too late to warm up before ballet class, which was an unpardonable sin to Madame Pershoff of the Corps de Ballet Dance Studio. Rachel barely had time to put on her pointe shoes and leg warmers before Madame started barre exercises.

Rachel could hardly remember her life before ballet. She'd been a student of Madame Pershoff's for eight years—ever since she was five years old. At first, it was just something for a cute little girl with bony knees and elbows to do for fun. But it wasn't long before Rachel knew deep down in her heart that she wanted to be a professional ballerina—more than anything in the world. And no one in Miami could prepare her for that life better than Madame Tasha Pershoff.

Sometimes Rachel hated the woman. Sometimes she loved her. But always, always, she respected her. And Madame Pershoff wouldn't have wasted her time on students she didn't think had real talent. Rachel knew if she wanted to realize her dream, then Madame Pershoff was the only one to help her.

"Rachel!" Madame Pershoff's sharp voice interrupted her thoughts. "Are you asleep? Your barre work is very poor today."

The words cut through Rachel, and she felt tears spring into her eyes. "I–I'm sorry," she stammered. Nothing was more embarrassing than being criticized before the entire class. Rachel felt her neck and face flush red.

The other girls froze in painful silence. They could all appreciate Rachel's agony.

"I–I just don't feel very well today." She hated herself for saying that. Madame Pershoff disliked complaints about physical problems.

"Then perhaps you should sit down."

"Oh, no. I–I'll be fine." Rachel felt like sliding through the floorboards.

Her instructor glared at her a moment longer, then nodded to the pianist. Miss Lucy began again. "One and two and up and down . . ." Madame Pershoff started in her thick accent.

It's no use, Rachel thought miserably. *I'm just not with it today. And I HAVE to go to the bathroom.* She caught Madame's eye and motioned towards the door. Then Rachel left the barre and slipped into the tiny dressing room.

School clothes cluttered the floor. Shirts, jeans, shoes, and books lay in piles and jumbles. Each of Madame Pershoff's advanced dance students had hurried in from the hot, late-September afternoon and changed into leotards, tights, and pointe shoes.

Two hours. For as long as Rachel could remember, two hours every day. Four hours on Saturdays. Rehearse. Practice. Except when a dance concert was planned. Then classes were even longer and more demanding.

And Rachel knew that with Christmas coming up, Madame Pershoff would be planning another concert, a performance to showcase her top students. Rachel's heart skipped in anticipation. The performances—that's what made it all worthwhile. To go out on a stage and dance. And then to hear the applause. It was the most exciting feeling in the world! Weeks and weeks of practice for one glorious moment on the stage.

Rachel hurried to the bathroom and then slipped back into the class. *Darn!* she thought again. *I should have gotten a drink.* She had been so thirsty lately. Ever since her bout with the flu two weeks before, Rachel had been feeling lousy. She forced herself to concentrate on the exercises.

Madame Pershoff halted the exercises—finally—and began working with the girls in pairs. Rachel was glad she was at the far end of the barre.

Rachel glanced into the mirror only to see the cool blue eyes of Melanie Hallick staring back at her. She quickly looked away, hoping Melanie wouldn't realize that she wasn't up to par.

Darn her anyway, Rachel thought. Beautiful, talented Melanie. Always competing with Melanie for the best dance parts in Madame Pershoff's concerts. Cold, aloof Melanie. Always giving the impression that she was above them all.

Oh, they'd been attending the same dance classes for years. They even had a class together at school this year. But Melanie was a loner. Rachel had given up being friendly to her years before. But why did she have to be so pretty?

Melanie was a classic beauty, Rachel had to admit. Her features reminded Rachel of something the Romans once carved on the front of their temples. Pale blond hair; fine, high cheekbones; ice-blue eyes. She was perfectly proportioned, dainty, fine-boned. Melanie wasn't a hair over five-feet-four, while Rachel was a good five-foot-seven. It was awful to be so tall and thin sometimes. True, her height did help her look graceful on the dance floor. But it wasn't much fun being the tallest girl in the entire eighth grade at Miami Junior High School.

I wonder if she ever giggles? Rachel brooded. Then she remembered that Melanie had giggled once—at Rachel, when she'd been paired off with Skip Schuster as a debate partner. He'd been a whole four inches shorter than Rachel! How silly they must have looked. Couldn't teachers see differences in height? Miss Perfect had gotten Brandon Mitchell for a partner. Brandon was only the cutest boy in the school. And he was at least five-foot-nine. Short, pretty Melanie had gotten Brandon as her partner, and tall, skinny Rachel had gotten Skip.

Rachel glanced up at the clock. Five o'clock. Another half hour to go. And she had to go to the bathroom again. Well, she just wasn't going to fight it anymore today.

Rachel stole back into the dressing room and tugged off her dance gear. She slipped on her faded jeans and sandals and took out the pins that held her short brown hair off her forehead. Madame Pershoff thought all dancers should have long hair worn in a bun. But Rachel didn't like the bother of long hair. And she thought long hair made her look as young as her little sister, Chris.

Rachel brushed her hair quickly. She wanted to get out of there before the class was dismissed. She just didn't feel like standing around talking with the other girls today.

"I hope Mom's early," she said aloud as she picked up her books and ballet bag and hurried down the narrow flight of stairs to the street below. Of course, her mom wasn't there.

Rachel looked both ways down the crowded Miami sidewalk. No familiar blue car was waiting at the curb. She sighed and slumped down on the bus bench. Well, she was early. Still she felt irritated at her mother. It was hot. It was always hot this time of year in Miami. And it would be hot for another two months.

I wonder what it would be like to live where it snows, she thought. *A white Christmas*. Rachel decided to slip into the drugstore and get a Coke. The air conditioning felt refreshing.

"Well, well, how do you do today, Miss Rachel?" Mr. Santos asked her.

"Just fine," she lied.

"You should take it easy. You look very tired—there are dark circles under your eyes," he scolded gently.

Swell! she thought. *Now I look like a raccoon*. She forced a smile at him and took the paper cup back out to the bus bench.

Just in time. Her mother's car halted in front of her. Rachel opened the door and slid onto the seat.

"How'd it go today, honey?" her mother asked.

"Just fine." Rachel thumped her books down on the floor at her feet and quickly opened up her history book. Maybe if she started reading, her mother wouldn't start talking. And she could ignore the fact that she still needed to go to the bathroom. It worked.

Mrs. Deering concentrated on the traffic, and the ride home was finished in silence. When the car had barely stopped, Rachel darted out of it and hurried up the winding walk and into air-conditioned house.

She made it to the bathroom just in time. Then Rachel headed for the comfort and privacy of her bedroom.

Everything was pale pink and ivory. Her canopy bed and rose-colored carpet were perfect! It had been fun redoing the room for her thirteenth birthday last summer. She lay across the bed and stared over at her posters of Mikhail Baryshnikov and Suzanne Farrell. Dancers' bodies were so beautiful. Long legs, well-proportioned muscles, graceful necks, slender arms, and proud heads.

Rachel reached over to turn on her stereo. But her *Swan Lake* CD was gone! She sat up angrily. Chris! Darn her!

Rachel bolted out of her room and down the hall to Chris's room. The little brat was not there.

"Mom!" Rachel yelled, hurrying into the kitchen. There sat her nine-year-old sister helping her mother make a salad. "Mom, Chris went into my room again. Without my permission!"

"Did not!" Chris countered.

"She took my CD," Rachel snapped. "I want a lock for my door."

"Now, girls, stop it. I don't want your father coming in to all this fussing and fighting."

"Ouch!" Chris yelped. "She hit me!"

"Rachel!" Mrs. Deering snapped. "Now stop it! Chris, don't go into your sister's room without permission. And Rachel, stop hitting Chris."

"Well, she deserved it."

"I bought you that CD for your birthday. I like to listen to it, too," Chris sulked.

Rachel glared at her. Skinny little brat. Even after two years of dance classes with Pershoff, Chris lacked the grace and form that Rachel had developed.

Rachel retreated to her room again and lay across the bed sulking. She was thirsty. The Coke had only made her even thirstier. And she was hungry, too. What a rotten day!

Maybe she'd call Jenny. Maybe something was happening that would make Rachel feel better. She and Jenny had been best friends since second grade, and in fact, Jenny was her only real friend. Jenny didn't dance a step, but they had managed to have everything else in common. Besides, Jenny was a real clown. She cracked us all up with her imitation of the principal, Mrs. Brady. Jenny the clown and Rachel the dancer. What a combination!

Sometimes Rachel envied the easy way Jenny made friends, the way she could become the center of attention by making a crazy face or dropping a hilarious one-liner. Then Rachel frowned, remembering how different things had been between them since Ben had come along.

Ben Cole had made a beeline for Jenny on the first day of school in September. And he hadn't let her out of his sight since. At first, Jenny let him tag along, but over the weeks he became so much a part of Rachel and Jenny's times together that Rachel could hardly recall Life Before Ben. Naturally, Rachel had been hurt a little as Jenny became more and more attached to Ben. But then Rachel's life had been so consumed with ballet that she could hardly blame Jenny for turning to Ben.

Besides, Ben was sort of cute, and he and Jenny made a fun combination. *I wonder what it would be like to have a boyfriend,* Rachel thought. She walked over to her full-length mirror and gave herself a good, hard look.

"Dark brown hair, brown eyes . . . pretty ordinary," she said aloud. Still, she did have the unmistakable carriage of a dancer: straight back, arms that hung gracefully at her sides, the slightly outward-turned feet that sometimes gave her a duck-like walk. "Well, I'm no beauty," she said with a sigh.

Still, what would it be like to be kissed? Had Ben kissed Jenny yet? Rachel puckered up her lips and closed her eyes. But all she could conjure up was Ben. No, no. That wouldn't do. Brandon! Wow. What would it be like to kiss Brandon?

Her thoughts were interrupted by a tap on her door.

"Yes?" she said sheepishly, heading for the door.

"Rachel, it's me," her mother said. "Madame Pershoff just called. I need to speak with you."

Rachel opened the door and her mother came inside.

"Madame Pershoff said you left class early today."

Why did her mother always make her feel defensive? "I was thirsty. I didn't leave *that* early," Rachel finished.

"Honey, I don't care," said Nancy Deering in that voice that meant, "I *do* care." "Anyway, she said that you missed her announcement about this year's dance concert. She's holding it downtown at the old Olympus Theater. She hopes that an old friend of hers will be there from an important ballet school. Oh, Rachel, she's only asking her four best students to try out for the lead. She wants you, Pat, Melanie, and Jill to prepare for the dying swan solo in *Swan Lake*, and she'll choose one of you. Oh, Rachel! Isn't it exciting? I know you can get the part."

Rachel felt her heart leap. *Swan Lake*! Every ballerina's dream! She could imagine herself in the satiny costume, the layered skirt, the feathered headpiece. The stage. The lights. And the music! Pat and Jill—they shouldn't be too hard to beat out. But Melanie! That was going to be a challenge.

"Oh, Mom," Rachel said, jumping up from her bed, "I want that part. More than anything—I want that part!"

-TWO-

"Rachel, for goodness sake," said Mr. Deering. "Take it easy! That's the third glass of orange juice you've gulped down this morning."

Rachel glanced over at her father and smiled half-heartedly. "Sorry," she mumbled. "I'm just extra thirsty today." She still felt terrible, but she didn't want her parents to know. They might make her stay home from school, and if she didn't go to school, she couldn't go to dance class. She'd been planning to attend extra night classes since she'd learned about the *Swan Lake* part.

After all, she'd barely practiced at all yesterday, so she had a lot of making up to do. Rachel buttered her toast and glanced over at her dad. She always thought he was the most handsome man in the world. Richard Deering was tall, distinguished, and slightly graying at his temples. Rachel bet he was the best lawyer in Miami.

Rachel's mom came into the dining room. "Honey, don't you want more eggs?"

"No, thanks," Mr. Deering said.

"Where's Chris?" Mrs. Deering asked Rachel.

"No idea," Rachel murmured.

Just then Chris ran breathlessly into the room.

"You're late," her mother scolded.

"Well, Rachel *hogged* the bathroom all morning—"

"I did *not*!" Rachel shot back.

"Now, girls . . . ," their father began.

"Rachel, you've been spending a lot of extra time in there lately," Mrs. Deering said. "Are you feeling all right?"

"Well, of course, I am." Rachel shot an angry glance at her sister. "I've got to go now. Don't want to be late. Bye, Dad." She kissed his forehead. "Bye, Mom." She snatched her books and darted out the front door before they had time to react.

It was a short walk to the bus stop, and she was already tired before she got there. What was wrong with her anyway?

The cafeteria was noisy as usual. Rachel sat there pushing the food around on her tray. Ugh! Sloppy Joes—greasy and completely unappetizing. She'd already finished her milk, but she was still thirsty.

"Want your juice?" she asked Jenny.

Naturally, Ben was talking with Jenny, so her friend never even heard the question. Still, Rachel had to smile at the thought of Jenny's most recent imitation of Mrs. Brady giving fire drill instructions.

Suddenly she heard the unmistakable voice of Brandon Mitchell. She looked up to meet his brown eyes squarely. She felt herself blushing and looked back down quickly. *Oh, no,* she thought. *He saw me staring at him*! But if he did, he didn't show it. Instead he walked directly over to Melanie, who was nibbling on her lunch and reading a book.

Rachel watched them. They looked good together. Pretty Melanie, smiling up at Brandon. Brandon sat down across from Melanie and leaned over to whisper something to her. She laughed out loud. Then Rachel could swear that they both looked over at her. She blushed again.

That did it! They were talking about her for sure. She stood up quickly and yanked her lunch tray up. But when she spun toward the dirty tray window, the tray slipped from her hands.

CRASH! The noise echoed throughout the cafeteria. And all life stopped. Every eye in the entire cafeteria turned to stare at Rachel. She wished she could die. Brandon and Melanie. Jenny and Ben. It seemed that every person in the whole school was staring at her. Rachel fled, tears welling up in her eyes.

She stopped in the bathroom and splashed cold water on her burning face. She tried to get a grip on her nerves. What was wrong with her? People dropped lunch trays every day. She gathered her courage and headed for Mr. Levenson's science class.

Rachel stood at the barre, deep in concentration. *Plié* . . . first, second, and fifth positions. *Battements tendus . . . battements dégagés . . .*

ronds de jambe en l'air . . . over and over Rachel performed the familiar exercises. Then she moved into center floor practice. The same movements, this time without the barre, over and over.

She tried to keep her mind blank. Form, position, extension, stretch. *Try not to think about the day. Keep time with the music. Up and stretch.* In spite of the way she felt physically, Rachel knew that her barre exercises were flawless. The open admiration in the eyes of the younger girls told her so, too. She finished her class, changed, and gathered up her things. She headed for the door.

"Rachel!" her smug, good feelings were chased away by the sound of Madame Pershoff's voice. Rachel froze.

"Y—yes?" she stammered, catching her breath.

The frail woman leaned heavily on her silver-headed cane. "I wish to speak with you."

Silently Rachel followed her into her cramped office. The walls were filled with photos of a young, smiling ballerina in various classical dance poses. There were many other photos of familiar ballet stars, signed: "To Tasha . . ." "Best Wishes . . ." "Good Luck . . ." Rachel had often wondered what terrible accident had halted Tasha Pershoff's soaring career and how she had come to settle here in Miami.

Madame sat down in her swivel desk chair and motioned Rachel toward the old sofa. "I watched your barre work today," she began. Rachel stiffened. "It is very good." Rachel almost sighed. "But, I wonder . . . how is it that you feel?"

"What?" Rachel tried to sort out the woman's words. "Oh, I'm okay. I've been tired lately. Ever since I had the flu. But I'm better today."

"This concert," Madame continued. "I expect good things from you. I will have a friend there. He is most important for a dancer's career. Of all my students, you and Melanie show the most promise. You do want a future in ballet, yes?"

"Oh, yes!" Rachel cried. "More than anything! Dancing is my whole life."

"Oh, no, my dear," the silver-haired woman said. "You do not know yet what dedication is. But you will. You will. Now, no more today. You come to tomorrow's class prepared to *work*. Because there is much preparation before the tryouts. I need you here every day, working very hard."

After Rachel left the office, she was puzzled. Why had Madame Pershoff given her the pep talk anyway? Maybe there was a lot more going on than just the annual Christmas concert. Who was this friend of hers? Had she said the same things to Melanie? Was she trying to keep them competitive? No, for some reason, this upcoming showcase was very special to Madame Pershoff. Very special indeed.

"I'm telling you it's impossible!" Jenny wailed into Rachel's ear through the phone receiver. "I'm too young to spend the rest of my life chained to a history book. I mean, who cares what the Romans did? Doesn't Mrs. Matthews know that there's more to life than who-ruled-Rome-when?"

Rachel half-heard her through her haze. She was so tired. Much too tired to listen to Jenny prattle on. But it was only eight-thirty, and Rachel really didn't want to go to bed yet. Besides, she hadn't finished her homework.

"Uh, Jen, I've got to go. Chris is begging for the phone. And you know how that goes."

"Oh, yeah, sure. See you in homeroom."

Rachel felt a little guilty about her white lie. She went into the bathroom and splashed cold water on her face. She felt flushed, and her complexion looked a little pink in the mirror. *Oh, I can't get sick,* she thought. *I just have to make dance class from now on.*

"Are you in the bathroom *again*?" Chris's voice cut through her thoughts.

"Oh, go away!"

"Well, every time I go by the door, you're in there."

"So what? You got the toilet paper concession?" Rachel shot back at her.

"Mom!" Chris shouted. "Rachel's talking mean to me."

Mrs. Deering materialized from out of nowhere. "Now what?"

Suddenly, Rachel felt too tired even to argue. "It's nothing. I think I'll go to bed early tonight."

"Honey, are you feeling all right?"

"Good grief, yes," Rachel snapped. "Can't I just go to bed early if I want?"

"Rachel, let's go into your room. I want to talk to you a minute," her mother said.

Rachel tossed herself across her bed and braced for her mother's lecture. Mrs. Deering closed the door behind her and stared at her daughter.

"Rachel . . . ," she started. "Honey, Dad and I are concerned about you."

"What for?"

"You just look so tired lately. And you've been drinking so much . . . and the bathroom routine—"

"Oh, Mother."

"I mean it, Rachel. We think you may be pushing yourself too hard. After all, eighth grade is a big adjustment in itself without all the dance classes."

"Well, I won't stop dancing!" she cried defensively.

"No one is asking you to stop," her mother said soothingly. "But your father and I both want you to go by Dr. Stein's office tomorrow right after school. You can still make ballet class," she finished quickly.

"Dr. Stein! The *baby* doctor?"

"Rachel, he's a pediatrician. You've been seeing him for years."

"But that's when I've needed shots or something. I don't want to go to a baby doctor. Especially when I'm perfectly fine."

"No, Rachel, there will be no arguing about this. I've already made the appointment. I'll pick you up at two-thirty and drop you off at his office. Then I have to take Chris down to the dance store for new ballet shoes. If you finish early, you can catch the number six bus to ballet class. I won't embarrass you by sitting in his office with you. I've already told him some of your symptoms, and Dr. Stein wants to see you. He'll probably do some tests, and you'll be out in no time. He'll phone if there's anything wrong."

Rachel knew by the finality in her mother's voice that there was no use fighting about it. She would have to see Dr. Stein. After her mother left the room, Rachel felt like crying.

Why did they treat her like a baby? Madame Pershoff considered her a top ballet student, accomplished enough to perform in an important concert for "an important friend." But her own parents still thought of her as a little kid.

"I can't wait 'til I'm grown up!" she said aloud. "I'll have my own apartment with no one telling me what to do."

She went to the bathroom one more time and then returned to her soft bed, where she fell into a fitful sleep.

-THREE-

"You smell funny." Chris wrinkled her nose in Rachel's direction at the breakfast table.

"Thanks a lot," Rachel countered dully. She felt so tired. Too tired to argue even.

"Did you put on fingernail polish in the middle of the night? I'll bet you did!" Chris added.

Rachel held up her unpainted nails and dangled them under Chris's nose. "See, smarty. No polish."

Chris sat back and gobbled down her cereal. Rachel felt sick to her stomach. She couldn't face her breakfast, so she drank her juice and gathered up her books. "Bye, Mom . . . Dad. I'm headed for the bus stop."

"Just a minute," her mother called and followed her to the front door. "Now, don't forget. I'll pick you up at two-thirty sharp by the front entrance. Then I'll drop you off at Dr. Stein's."

"I'll be waiting," Rachel said crossly.

She walked the two blocks to her bus stop. It was a beautiful October day, and the air smelled pure and fresh. Two months until Christmas. It didn't seem possible. Only two months to practice until the concert.

I'm going to have to feel a lot better soon, when I get that part instead of Melanie, she told herself. Madame Pershoff didn't play favorites. The best talent always got the role. Sometimes Rachel won them . . . sometimes Melanie. But this was one part Rachel intended to have.

Frankly, she was glad in a way that she was going to the doctor's. Even if it was Dr. Stein. She really had been feeling rotten lately. She'd noticed that morning that she'd lost four pounds since last week. And she'd been eating like a horse, too.

Why, when she'd put on her top that morning, she could count most of her ribs! And the dark circles under her eyes—she had cheated. She'd put on some of her stage makeup to cover them up. She'd known that her parents would never have let her go to school if they had seen how bad she looked.

"Hi. Knew that was you coming," Jenny called. "You always walk so straight. Honestly, I look like I have curvature of the spine next to you. What's wrong?"

"Oh, nothing. I don't feel so hot today."

"You don't look so hot either. Maybe you should go back home. Wish I could. Talked to Ben half the night instead of studying. Sure hope I don't have any pop quizzes today. At the rate I'm going, I'll be repeating eighth grade for sure."

Rachel listened to Jenny go on and on. But she didn't feel much like talking back. She hoped she'd feel better by ballet class.

The day dragged on and on. Rachel's thirst was unquenchable. She drank water before class and after, but her thirst was so intense that it hurt. And the bathroom visits were even more urgent than before. And she felt like she was going to be sick. By lunchtime Rachel was afraid she wouldn't make it through the day.

She was climbing the stairs to her one o'clock class when she got so woozy that she staggered. Strong hands grabbed her from the back.

"You all right?"

Rachel turned and looked into the brown eyes of Brandon Mitchell. He held her arm and steadied her against the wall.

"I–I think so," she mumbled.

"I think you should go to the clinic," he said and helped her walk toward the office.

She felt too weak to protest. And Brandon's guiding hands felt so strong. She didn't even feel embarrassed. It was nice to have him help her. Deep inside she wished Melanie could see her now.

The nurse took over from Brandon in the clinic. She made Rachel lie down. Rachel heard the tardy bell ring, but she couldn't have cared less. "I can call your mother," the nurse offered.

"No, that's okay. She's picking me up at two-thirty anyway. Maybe if I just lie here for a while . . ."

"Fine. Let me know if you need anything."

By two-thirty, Rachel did feel better, a little stronger and more rested. She took a long drink, thanked the nurse, and headed toward the entrance to meet her mother.

The halls were teeming with kids, and Rachel thought she saw Brandon. She wanted to thank him, but suddenly she felt very shy. He'd helped her. Put his arm around her! She couldn't wait to tell Jen. Well, maybe she wouldn't. Jen was used to having a boy put his arm around her. It would be no big deal to her.

"Rachel!" Her mother called from the car. Rachel forced a smile on her face as she got inside, and they rode in silence to the doctor's office.

"Now, here are your leotard, tights, and ballet shoes," her mother said as Rachel got out at Dr. Stein's office. "If I'm not back when you're ready to go to class, just catch the bus. Do you have the fare?"

"Yes, Mother," Rachel sighed. And then, dreading every minute of it, she went into the air-conditioned building.

Babies! Crying, gurgling, climbing . . . the office was full of babies and toddlers.

"Anthony! Stop that!" an impatient women called to a little boy who was teasing his sister.

The racket made Rachel's head hurt all the more. She couldn't wait until this was over. She signed in at the nurse's window.

"Well, hi, Rachel," said Miss Wimberly with a smile. "Look, it's going to be a while. As you can see, we're knee-deep in business. Why don't you wait in the older children's waiting room?" She motioned toward another door.

"Wait!" Rachel exclaimed. "I have ballet class. I can't wait long."

"Oh, it won't be that long. And I know Dr. Stein wants to see you. How about giving us a urine sample before you sit down?"

After Rachel turned in her sample, she took a seat in the waiting room for older kids. It wasn't half as full. But after twenty minutes she began to fidget. What was taking so long?

She was starting to feel a little sick to her stomach again. But she had to make ballet class. Madame Pershoff was expecting her. She just had to practice for that part.

She watched the clock. It was 3:15. The bus came at 3:20. It was a thirty-minute ride from Dr. Stein's office to the studio.

If I leave right now, I can make class on time, she told herself. Sure, her parents would be mad, but it wasn't her fault that Dr. Stein was so busy. Besides, if she told the nurse she was leaving, they'd only try to talk her into staying. *No*, she decided. *I can come back tomorrow. I'm sure I'll live another day.*

The bus was early and made good time. She had a full fifteen minutes to dress for class at the studio. It was just as well, too. She was feeling awfully weak.

"You don't look like you're sick." The voice was Melanie's. Rachel looked up from her struggle with her pink tights into Melanie's cool, blue eyes.

"I feel fine now," Rachel lied.

"Yes, Brandon told me he had to help you to the clinic. That you almost passed out in the hall."

Rachel hated the accusing sound in Melanie's voice. As if she'd been faking it! As if she'd thrown herself at Brandon instead of almost fainting! Suddenly she hated Melanie Hallick. She turned back to pulling on her tights and hurriedly put on her leotard and ballet shoes. She went out into the studio determined to do her very best. She was going to get that part if it killed her! She'd show Melanie a thing or two.

Rachel took her place at the barre. She began stretching exercises and felt a wave of dizziness come over her. She gripped the barre for support and cautiously looked around. Good. No one had noticed. But her legs felt kind of rubbery, and she took deep breaths, trying to regain her composure.

Tears of frustration sprang to her eyes. Why was this happening to her? All she wanted to do was feel good and dance her very best. All she had ever wanted to be was a ballerina. And now, at thirteen, she was close to obtaining her goal. By fifteen, she could be in a ballet corps with a famous company like the Ballet Russe de Monte Carlo or the New York City Ballet. They were always looking for young, promising dancers.

And by seventeen, she might even be dancing solo parts. If she was good enough, she might even get a dance scholarship to an important ballet school. True, Madame Pershoff was good, but Rachel knew that someday she would have to move on if she wanted to become a ballerina. And she had to keep working at her goal!

Rachel gritted her teeth and concentrated on her barre work. *Relevé . . . plié . . .* again . . . stretch . . . bend . . . again. In the mirror, she saw Melanie take her place at the barre. She heard other girls go past her to take their positions. She saw everything as if it were moving in slow motion.

The floor—why was it tilting? *That's strange,* she thought, *the barre is wrinkled.* Pinpoints of light burst behind her eyes, and she felt herself sinking to the floor. But she had no control over her own body.

Vaguely she could hear people yelling . . . voices calling her name, "Rachel . . . Rachel!" Over and over. Hands touching her. Blackness engulfing her. Always the voices. And from somewhere, the sound of running feet.

A siren wailed. Strong hands lifted her onto something that rolled. A man's fingers forced open her eyelids. A bright light pierced her vision. A tight squeezing on her arm. And voices. She had to get up. No, she couldn't. She was being lifted into the back of a . . . car?

A truck . . . an ambulance? "Why?" she asked. "Sh–h–h," voices said.

They were pushing her down a hall. Lights zoomed by overhead. A large room. More faces. Men and women in white coats and . . . doctors? Nurses? "I want my mother."

"BP . . . temp . . . pulse."

"She's dehydrated. Get the IVs hooked up."

"Smell that acetone?"

More voices. "Lab? Blood stat. Give me those numbers."

Pricks on her arm . . . so tired . . . pricks on the backs of her hands. Metal clanking. There was a long tube and a plastic bag hanging by her head.

She could smell alcohol. "ICU . . . Get her on monitors. BP every thirty . . ."

"I'm cold." She was falling. She was fighting not to sleep. The sounds were fading. The voices were far away. Everything was swimming into blackness . . . then there was nothing.

-FOUR-

"**W**ell, young lady, welcome back to the real world." The first thing Rachel saw when she opened her eyes was the face of a man dressed in white. He had perfectly groomed, sandy blond hair and a neatly trimmed beard. He smiled down at her and said, "I'm Dr. Malar. You're in the hospital and you've been a pretty sick girl. But you're going to be all right."

"Where are my mom and dad?" she asked weakly.

"Right outside the door," he assured her. "I'll get them."

When her parents entered, Rachel couldn't believe how tired and worried they looked. Her mother hugged her tightly. Rachel could see that her eyes were brimming with tears. "Hi, honey," her father said gruffly. "Dr. Malar said you're going to be fine."

Rachel felt very confused. Vaguely she remembered strange voices and bright lights and odd smells. "What happened to me?" she asked weakly.

Her parents glanced knowingly at each other. Dr. Malar stepped forward and took hold of her free hand. The other one was pinned to her hospital bed with a tube running out of it.

"The technical term is ketoacidosis. It's the last stage of the disease diabetes mellitus."

"What?" Rachel asked. "What are you talking about? Am I going to die?"

"Goodness, no," Dr. Malar said quickly. "But you've got a lot to learn over the next week or so. Right now, get some rest. We can talk more later."

Questions. She had a hundred questions. But suddenly she was very tired. She did feel better knowing she wasn't going to die. Yet the look on her parents faces told her they weren't nearly as convinced as the doctor.

"Two days?" Rachel asked. "You mean I've been here two days already?" It was evening, and Dr. Malar sat on her bed flipping through a chart with her name on it.

"That's right," he confirmed. "Diabetic acidosis is very serious. It often leads to coma. But we've got you stabilized now. In fact, tomorrow morning I'm going to put you on real food instead of just that liquid stuff dripping into your hand." He motioned toward the IV.

"When can I go home?" she asked.

"Whoa, lady," he said, smiling. "First things first. You've got a lot of things to learn over the next week . . . maybe even ten days."

"But school . . . a–and my ballet classes—"

"Don't worry. You'll be doing all those things soon enough. But first you've got to learn how to take care of yourself. You're going to meet a lot of people during the next few days. A dietician. My associate, Ann Simon. Nurses. Even some other kids with diabetes."

"But why? You said I was going to be fine."

"And you are. But diabetes is a life-long condition. You've got to learn to manage it. To control it. To take care of yourself. That's why we keep you here for a while. We want you to feel confident about taking care of yourself when you go home."

"How will I take care of myself?"

"Proper diet. Blood-sugar testing. Exercise. And naturally, daily insulin injections."

"Shots?" Rachel asked with a lurch forward. "You mean, I have to take shots *every day*?"

Dr. Malar nodded. "Twice a day," he said.

"Oh, but I can't! I won't!"

"Yes, you will," he said sternly. "You're a type 1 diabetic. That means that your pancreas has stopped manufacturing insulin altogether. And without insulin, all the food you eat can't be used by your cells. Look," he explained, "insulin acts like a little key. It opens the door of your cells and allows glucose—that's another name for sugar—to come in and be used by your cells as food. You don't make any more insulin. Therefore, all the food you were eating was being turned into glucose, but it had no place to go. So, it built up in your bloodstream. You were thirsty all the time, right?"

"Yes," she confirmed.

"And you went to the bathroom a lot?"

"Yes."

"That was your body's way of trying to flush out the glucose. That's why you kept losing weight. Your body started breaking down fat and protein for energy. You started building up acetone—you even smelled like the stuff. You know, fingernail polish remover? Finally, the job became too big and your system went into 'tilt' or ketoacidosis. You were very sick."

"But why can't I just take pills? Why shots?"

"Because pills are for people who make some insulin, but not enough. You don't make any. Daily injections are the only way to get insulin inside you. Twice-daily injections mean better control."

"But I just can't stick myself with a needle!" she whispered.

"Look," Dr. Malar countered, "there are over eighteen million diabetics in this country. Two hundred thousand of those are kids. And they all get shots. The majority give themselves their own injections. Because without insulin, you *will* die. It's as simple as that."

When her parents came to see her that night, Rachel's eyes were still red from crying. Why was this happening to her? It was so awful. Two weeks before, she'd been a normal thirteen-year-old girl. Now she was a freak—someone who needed shots and special diets and "managing."

Her parents looked very worn-out. But she didn't care. It was happening to her, not to them. How could they possibly understand?

"How did I get this thing?" she asked them. "Did I catch it from someone?"

"No," her mom began. "I've been doing some reading about it. It seems it's a hereditary illness. I can remember an aunt of mine having it. And Grandmother, too, for about five years before she died. But she was over eighty."

"The doctors say that there's a virus involved, too," her father added. "You have to have the genes for it, but a virus is involved."

"Well, I hate it!" Rachel cried out.

"Oh, honey, we know. We're so sorry."

"Do you know that I have to take insulin shots for the rest of my life?" she sobbed. "That I'm never going to get well?"

"Yes," her father said. "But Dr. Malar assured us that diabetics can lead normal lives. As long as you take care of yourself, you can do all the things you did before. Dr. Malar is a pediatric endocrinologist. The best in Miami. He's going to be supervising you and taking care of you."

"I don't care," Rachel said angrily. "I hate it! And it's all your fault that I have it!"

Rachel sat on the side of the bed and stared at the insulin syringe. The needle was very short, but it looked a foot long to her. Dr. Malar and his assistant, Ann, stood next to her.

Ann had shown her how to draw up the insulin into the syringe. How to thump out the air bubbles and check for accuracy. Ann had even drawn up a syringe of saline solution and injected it into herself.

No doubt to show me "it doesn't really hurt," Rachel thought sarcastically. But she asked aloud, "Will it hurt?"

"Yes," Dr. Malar answered. "Some. Insulin stings a little going in. But you'll get used to it. Try not to tense up. Take a couple of deep breaths. Relax the muscles in your leg. Exhale. Then inject the syringe."

With trembling fingers, Rachel pinched up the skin on her leg. She'd wiped it with alcohol three times, but she hadn't yet gotten up the courage to stab herself. Dr. Malar held the syringe over the spot. Suddenly she took a deep breath, exhaled, and plunged the needle into her leg.

Quickly she pushed down the plunger, pulled it out and pressed the alcohol swab over the site. It *had* stung. Tears welled up behind her eyes. But secretly she felt pretty pleased with herself.

"Good for you, Rachel!" Ann said.

"Very good," Dr. Malar confirmed. "I'll be back this evening before supper to supervise your next one. Believe me, the first one is always the hardest."

"How would you know?" Rachel said meanly. "It hurt—a *lot*."

Dr. Malar paused. Then he reached inside his shirt collar and tugged on a chain. It pulled free and a small metal disc with a red insignia dangled from his hand.

"This is a Medic Alert medallion. Anyone with any health problems should wear one at all time. Your mother has already ordered one for you. Please read mine."

He turned it over and held it close for her to see. *John L. Malar, Diabetes,* it said.

"I know," he told her. "I know very well, Rachel."

The dietician had just left. Rachel stared at the pile of papers she had been given. "Recipes for Better Diabetic Diets," "How to Eat Like a King on a Diabetic Diet," "Your Exchange Diet Plan—1,500 Calories." Her head was swimming. "Six saltines equals one bread exchange," she read aloud. "One medium apple equals one fruit exchange." It was all so confusing.

The dietician had told her it would be. She had said that she'd spent time with Rachel's mother, who was also learning all about a diabetic's diet needs.

No more French fries and Cokes after school! No more midnight ice cream pig-outs. Her life was going to be a nightmare. "This stinks," Rachel said aloud and flung the diet papers across the room.

"What's wrong, honey?" her mother asked as she came into the room.

"I've got diabetes," Rachel shot back.

"Now, honey . . . you're going to be all right. And besides, I've got some good news for you. Jenny and Ben have been calling daily. They want to come up and see you during visiting hours tonight. Dr. Malar said it would be fine."

"What!" Rachel squealed. "I don't want to see anybody! Do you hear, not anybody! I don't want anyone to know *ever* about my shots and diet. I'm a freak!"

"Rachel! Stop that! Your friends are concerned about you. They don't know much about diabetes. But they do care about you. And," Mrs. Deering took a deep breath, "Madame Pershoff wants to come see you, too."

Ballet. Her first love. "How can I even think about ever dancing again?" she asked her mother. "Oh, Mom, all I ever wanted to do was dance. But how can I now?" She began to cry.

"Oh, honey," Mrs. Deering put her arms around her daughter. "I know it will all work out. Dr. Malar says that regular exercise is part of good diabetic control. And dancing is good exercise. Don't cry, Rachel. We'll work something out. I promise. Now won't you please let me call your friends and tell them it's all right to come for a visit? I know it will make you feel better. Please?"

"Okay," she said. "I guess I have to face them sooner or later. But I don't want to see Madame Pershoff. Not yet, please."

"Boy, breakfast in bed . . . your own TV . . . people waiting on you hand and foot . . . not too bad, Rachel." Jenny flitted around the room pushing buttons and making funny faces. Ben stood off to one side looking uncomfortable.

"Sure, Jen," Rachel answered. "It's a regular hotel. Care to join me?"

"And miss out on a week of Matthews' history class? I couldn't stand that," Jenny said with a laugh.

Her mother had been right. It *was* good to see her friends again. And it made Rachel want to get out of the hospital, too. For the first time, she really began to long to go back home.

They talked on and on, sharing school stories and jokes. Finally the call came over the speaker system for visitors to leave. Jenny patted Rachel's hand good-bye. Ben barely brushed her fingers.

"Got to run," Jenny said and shot Ben a mean glance.

That's odd, Rachel thought. *It's like they're afraid to touch me.*

It wasn't until they had left the room that Rachel got an inkling of what was wrong. She could hear Jenny's voice outside the door. "For heaven's sake, Ben. You treated her like she had leprosy. Her mother told us that you can't 'catch' diabetes from Rachel like a cold. Honestly, you can be *so* insensitive."

-FIVE-

"Hi, there. You Rachel Deering?"

She looked up from her history book to see a tall boy standing in her hospital room doorway. He had dark red hair, a deep golden tan, and bright blue eyes. He was really cute.

Rachel self-consciously tugged the covers higher. "Yes," she answered.

"I'm Shawn McLaughlin. Dr. Malar sent me."

He eased into the room and pulled up a chair next to her bed. "He told me you were pretty. He's right."

Rachel blushed and looked away from his steady gaze. "What do you want?"

"Just thought I'd like to meet you. Thought you might like to meet someone who lives with diabetes every day."

"You have it, too?" She examined him openly. He seemed so . . . well. So healthy.

"Sure. Since I was three. I'm fourteen now. That's eleven years."

"Really?"

"Yep. And I hate having it as much as you do. But I've learned to live with it . . . around it . . . in spite of it," he said as he grinned broadly at her.

His smile was infectious. She smiled back.

"In a way," he continued, "I'm luckier than you. It happened to me when I was so young that I don't ever remember not having it. I've had two shots a day for forever, it seems. Let's see, three hundred sixty five times two . . . that's seven hundred thirty . . . . times eleven . . . that's eight thousand thirty . . . I forgot to count leap years in that. Yep, you could say 'I have it, too.'"

Rachel stared wide-eyed. "You talk about it so—so casually. Doesn't it bother you?"

"Sometimes. But I don't let it interfere with everything I want to do. I play soccer."

"You do?"

"Sure. At first, my folks started me playing to help control my blood sugar. But pretty soon I loved the game so much that I played in spite of my diabetes. I'm on the select team now. Really competitive play. We get to travel and play in championship matches. How about you?

Do anything special? Besides studying?" He glanced at her open book.

"No . . . I–I mean, I used to dance. Ballet. But now I don't know if I will again."

"Why?"

Just then she hated his intense eyes, like they could see right through her. It wasn't any of his business anyway.

He sensed her instant hostility. "Listen," he said as he got up and turned toward the door. "I'm not prying, believe me. I really just wanted you to know there are a lot of us diabetics out there. In fact, a group of about fifteen of us meet twice a month with Malar to talk. Share our problems. We have a pretty good time. Sometimes we have bowling parties or go swimming. It's good to get with other kids with the same problems. Maybe you'd like to meet with us sometime?"

She felt very uncomfortable under his gaze. Why did he have to be so cute? "No," she said quickly, "I don't think so."

"Well, if you change your mind, let Malar know. He's a pretty regular guy. For a doctor," Shawn said with a grin.

"I don't want to be reminded about my diabetes," Rachel explained. "Why would I want to sit around and talk about it with a bunch of strangers?"

"It's kind of like Alcoholics Anonymous for diabetics. Believe me, Rachel . . . it does help."

"Well, thanks anyway." She resented his intrusion into her life.

He smiled broadly. "I'll keep in touch." Then he was gone.

Darn Dr. Malar anyway! Who did he think he was? Shoving people down her throat. Well, maybe she did have diabetes, and maybe there was nothing she could do about it, but she was not going to accept it. Never! She would hate diabetes every single minute for the rest of her life!

"So you didn't think too much of Shawn?" Dr. Malar leaned back in the chair next to her bed.

Rachel had just finished giving herself her evening injection. "Oh, no. He was very nice—" she started.

"But you don't like to be reminded of the realities of your life," the doctor finished.

"I know I have diabetes," she said, defending herself.

"That's right, Rachel. You do. And you've been having quite a pity party over it."

"What?"

"You heard me. You're angry. Mad at your parents. They passed on the lousy genes. You're mad at me. 'How dare I change your life!' You're even mad at God. 'How dare He do this to you.'"

She avoided his eyes. He was right.

"Rachel, I can't make it go away. If it's any help, there are tremendous strides being made in research to find a cure. But for right now, it's daily injections, diet control, and urine and blood-sugar testing."

"Yes, I–I know. I'm doing my urine tests. I even did a Chemstrip today and found out that my blood sugar was about one hundred eighty."

"Good. Because controlling your blood sugar is the name of the game. I want you to feel good. I'll be regulating your insulin dose for a while. But pretty soon, you'll be able to decide if you need a little more insulin—like when you get sick. Or a little less—like when you exercise heavily."

"I want to go home. But I'm scared," she told him.

"I know. It's a lot to learn. But I want you to resume your normal life. School, dancing, dating. That won't change. But there will be adjustments. The important thing is to keep you feeling good, to keep you out of insulin reactions."

"Reactions?" she asked, surprised. "What's that?"

After he told her, Rachel was sorry she'd asked.

"As long as you take your insulin and follow the rules, you should never have to face acidosis again. But insulin reactions—they're part of diabetes."

"I don't understand."

"Well, sometimes you'll exercise more heavily than usual. You'll use up a lot of food at once. But your insulin level is still the same. With insulin floating around and nothing for it to react with, you'll experience a reaction. You may feel lightheaded. Or dizzy. You turn pale and shaky. Sometimes you might be nauseous or headachy. The first thing to do is reach for a fast-acting sugar—orange juice, candy, or sugar cubes. Always carry something sweet with you, just in case. Take it the minute you feel the symptoms coming on. Then eat something. Crackers, cheese, milk. You'll be fine in about ten minutes."

"What will happen if I don't?"

"You can pass out. Go into a coma. End up in the hospital. But, as long as you treat a reaction the minute it starts, you'll be all right."

The full horror of the information came over her. "It sounds so scary," Rachel said weakly. "There's so much to learn."

"Don't worry," said Dr. Malar. "You know all the main things already. In fact, I'm thinking of sending you on home day after tomorrow. We need to make room for sick people."

"It's going to be so good to have you home again, Rachel." Her mother chattered on and on as they packed her suitcase to leave the hospital.

"Dr. Malar says you can return to school on Monday. Won't it be good to get back to a normal life?"

Rachel listened half-heartedly. She was scared. In the hospital things were safe. There were people to take care of her. Nurses to interpret test results. Dieticians to figure out what she could eat. Doctors to help and protect her. At home and in school, she'd be on her own.

"So, what did you think of that nice boy, Shawn?" Mrs. Deering interrupted Rachel's thoughts.

"Huh? Oh, he was okay."

"I thought he was kind of cute," her mother added.

"I thought he acted like a know-it-all," Rachel said defensively.

"Well, your father and I really liked his parents. In fact, we're planning on attending meetings with them. There's a big Diabetes Research Institute here in Miami that's doing a lot of research to find a cure for diabetes. Parents of diabetics meet there monthly. Your dad and I both think we want to get involved." She paused, then went on. "You know, Marge

McLaughlin told me that there's a youth group that meets, too. Shawn's in it. These kids are all diabetics. Think you'd like to meet with them?"

Why was her mother pushing this stuff down her throat? "Not really," Rachel retorted. "I'd just as soon forget I even have diabetes. And I don't want to sit around and talk about it with a bunch of strangers. Shawn thinks he knows all about how I feel. Well, he doesn't. And neither do you. Nobody knows how I feel, and I hate everybody telling me that they understand."

Rachel hadn't thought she could miss the walls of her familiar bedroom so much. Her bed, her stereo, her posters . . . everything looked soft and pink and fresh. Her dad had even sent her a bouquet of pale pink rosebuds. The card read, "Welcome home, angel."

In a way, Rachel was even glad to see Chris. Oh, they'd let her come up to her hospital room—even though she was only nine—but Rachel hadn't thought about her sister too much during her hospitalization.

"And then Madame Pershoff asked me to do the combination. And I did it, Rachel! I mean, I didn't mess up *once*." Chris chattered away while they both sat at the kitchen table eating their snacks. Chris was wolfing down Oreos and milk while Rachel could only have saltines, cheese, and milk. Rachel hated it.

"You *are* going to class this afternoon, aren't you?" Chris asked her.

"Oh, I suppose I'll ride over there with you and Mom. But I won't be taking class for a while yet. Dr. Malar says I have to start back gradually. It will take a while to get really regulated." She almost choked on the words.

In almost every room of the house, subtle changes reminded her of her illness. In the bathroom, her urine testing equipment. In the kitchen, a shelf with syringes, alcohol swabs, and packages of Life Savers for her to carry.

The refrigerator held insulin, lots of protein foods, fresh fruit, and non-caloric drinks. She felt guilty that the entire family had to change their eating habits because of her.

"It will do us all good," her dad had said, but Rachel knew it would be a drag for them.

Still, she thought grimly, *Chris didn't have to give up Oreos.* And Rachel resentfully watched Chris gulp down her cookies.

The hardest part was walking up the long flight of stairs and into the dance studio. The familiar smells and sounds rushed to meet Rachel and sent a lump to her throat. Even though it was only a Saturday rehearsal, the feeling of Madame's iron discipline filled the hall. The long banks of mirrors reflected the legs and bodies of dancers in colorful leotards. Miss Lucy's piano played the familiar exercise pieces. It all made Rachel feel sad and lonely.

She longed to stretch on the barre, but she felt shy and afraid. Everyone glanced over at her. *They all know*, she thought. *They all know I'm sick.* Then she saw Melanie at the far end of the studio, standing off by herself, doing a graceful arabesque. How lovely she looked!

Lovely, Rachel thought bitterly. *And perfectly well. No illness for Melanie. Only perfect health.*

A perfect dancer's body. Rachel looked away, afraid that tears might brim over.

But her thoughts were interrupted by the sound of Madame Pershoff saying, "Rachel! How good to see you again! Come, come into my office right now. I must talk to you."

-SIX-

"Now sit down, here. Let me look at you." Madame motioned Rachel to the sofa in her cramped office, then sat down carefully in her swivel chair. She leaned forward on her silver-headed cane.

"I am so sorry about this thing that has happened to you. It is bad . . . I know this. But I also know that you can live with it. You are a strong girl. Do not let it take your mind off dance. I want to know when I can look for you again in class."

Rachel felt her stomach knot up. "I don't know." Her voice was so soft, Madame had to lean forward.

"So much has happened to me during the last two weeks," Rachel said. "I know that my doctor says that it is all right to dance. In fact, he wants me to continue. It's good for my control. But . . . well, I had serious plans once about dancing. Now I just don't know . . ." Her voice trailed off.

"Do not give up your dreams, Rachel. Look at you. Still you have a dancer's body and carriage. Still you have two legs that work." She paused, and Rachel knew that Madame's words must be painful for her to say. "Your life is not over. You can adjust. I know it. You still can dance . . . *if* you put your mind to it."

Rachel stared at Madame Pershoff. Once there had been a time when she would have given anything to hear what the old teacher was telling her now. Once those words would have filled her with confidence and pride and joy. But now . . . she was so confused and scared.

"I have many pupils," Madame continued. "Some are good. A few are very good."

"Like Melanie." Rachel spoke the words before she realized it.

"Yes." Madame nodded raising her eyebrows. "Like Melanie. She is good, Rachel. But—" Rachel's head shot up at the sharpness in her voice. "She is a technician. And that is important. Skill *is* involved. But you, Rachel . . . ah, you have the heart for the dance. The feeling, the spirit, the soul. This is something one is born with. One cannot learn it, no matter how many years one practices. Do you know what I am telling you?"

"I—I think so . . ."

"Come back to class. Naturally, it is too late for you and the Christmas concert. I have given the part to Melanie. But there will be other concerts—and parts for you. Come back to ballet. Some barre work . . . exercises. In no time you will be ready to be a full-time dancer. I feel you have a future. Please. Do not give up."

Rachel lay awake for a long time that night. She hadn't told anyone about Madame Pershoff's conversation. Whom could she share it with?

Her mother? Her sister? Even Jenny? No, none of them could possibly understand what she was going through. Of course she wanted to dance. She wanted to become a professional ballerina, but this diabetes had messed up her life so much.

It was as if a stranger had moved into her body. It was a part of her, yet it was an alien, too, running around inside her, pulling strings as if she were a puppet or something. "Don't eat this. Eat that. Get your shot. Beware of reactions." Would it always be like this?

She finally fell into a deep sleep and dreamed that she was looking into the window of an old house. All her friends were inside, laughing and eating and having a great time. Her parents were there, too. But she was locked out. She banged on the windows. But no one heard her. She shouted. But no one came over. She raced around to the front door and tried to get someone to open up and let her in. Suddenly a hand reached over and turned the doorknob. She watched the door swing open. She could still see all the party people having the time of their lives. But she was afraid to go inside. The hand that had opened the door for her took her gently by the elbow. She turned and looked up . . . into the smiling face of Shawn McLaughlin.

She was nervous her first day back at school. The last thing she wanted was everybody asking her a bunch of dumb questions. Rachel wanted everyone to just forget about her, to pretend that she'd only been out a few days with the flu or something. She didn't want them to think of her as different—or weird because she had to have insulin shots.

Jenny helped make her return easier. A few jokes and some funny faces, and by lunchtime the kids had forgotten that Rachel had even been gone a day. She was relieved and glad. She didn't want anything to remind her of her problems.

She took a long sip from her milk carton and glanced down the long lunch table at Brandon Mitchell. He was talking to a bunch of guys. He obviously didn't know that she was in the same room. But she knew he was there. If only she had the guts to go over and talk to him. She still owed him a "thank you" for helping her to the clinic that day.

If only she had Jenny's outgoing personality. It would be so easy to say something flip and cute. Wasn't anything ever going to go right in her life?

"Rachel, why is that perfectly gorgeous guy waving at you from the lunch line?" Jenny's voice interrupted Rachel's thoughts.

"What? Where?" Rachel squinted to see across the room. She saw a whole group of boys in uniforms of some sort standing with Mr. Perez, the PE coach. One kept waving at her. It was Shawn. He said something to the guy behind him and walked over to her seat.

"Hi. Thought that was you."

"What are you doing here?" Rachel asked.

"Our intramural soccer team is playing your school's team after school today."

She vaguely remembered hearing something about it over the speakers during announcements that morning. "Yes, of course . . ."

"So how goes it? Life back to normal yet?"

Darn him anyway! Rachel thought. *Why can't he just be quiet? Why remind everyone about me?*

Naturally, all movement had stopped around them, and Rachel felt like everyone in the school could hear them. "Everything's fine," she lied.

"Saw Dr. Malar yesterday. We're having a group meeting this Sunday. We were both wondering if you're coming."

"No . . . I don't think so. Would you excuse me? My lunch hour's up." She picked up her tray and tried to go by him.

He grinned down at her. "Why don't you come on out to the game today? We're going to stomp your team."

How arrogant! Suddenly she hated Shawn McLaughlin. Even if he was cute. All he did was remind her of all the things she wanted to forget. "No!" she called over her shoulder as she headed for the door and out onto the patio.

The sun was shining brightly but the air was cool, even for November in Florida. Rachel sat down heavily on the stone bench in the student courtyard. Kids milled around her, but she felt completely alone.

What a miserable day, she thought. *Of all the people to run into. Why him?* He made her very uncomfortable, looking at her as if he could see right through her, right into her private thoughts.

"You knew that gorgeous creature?" Jenny plopped down beside her.

"We—I mean, I met him in the hospital," Rachel answered.

Jenny shook her head at Rachel. "And you never said a word?" She sounded kind of hurt.

"He–he's got diabetes, too. My doctor sent him in to advise me," she added sarcastically.

"He likes you, Rachel."

"That's silly."

"No, I could see the way he was looking at you. Why aren't you going to the game this afternoon? Ben and I are going. You got ballet or something?"

"Yes. I mean, no. I'm not back dancing yet. I don't know. I just don't want to go."

"That's dumb. A really cute guy invites you to come watch him play soccer and you're too busy. Really dumb."

"Look, Jen," Rachel fumed. "I said I don't want to go. Now stop bothering me about it. I don't particularly like the guy. Cute or not."

The trouble with chorus was the size of the class. One hundred fifteen kids, seventh through ninth graders, all practicing in a small room during the last hour of the day. Sometimes Rachel wondered why she ever took chorus in the first place.

Spitballs sailed over her head. Jack Keegan kept snapping a ruler on the back of a chair.

Miss Hoggard was trying to regain control of the class. "Now, stop that this instant!" she yelled.

Rachel stared absently at her sheet music. Christmas songs. Normally she loved Christmas. But this year? No dance concert. No anything that meant something to her. Melanie would dance the Dying Swan solo. Well, at least Rachel didn't have to go and watch her.

"QUIET!" Miss Hoggard screamed at the top of her voice. Immediately every voice and sound stopped. "That's better," she continued calmly. "Now, class, turn to page four, measure two. Sopranos, you're in, then altos, then tenors. Basses, you're at least four beats off. Pay attention."

The piano began the familiar Christmas melody. For some reason it sounded far away to Rachel. She felt weak. Her hands started trembling! And suddenly she had such a headache. Her breath came in little gasps, and she felt faint.

"Are you all right?" Dianne asked next to her. "You look so pale."

Horrified, she knew what was happening to her. Insulin reaction! She'd been so flustered by

Shawn's appearance that she hadn't finished her lunch. And now—now she was so weak and sick.

"M–my purse . . . ," she said to Dianne through white, trembling lips.

By this time, the entire soprano section knew something was wrong.

"Girls!" Miss Hoggard snapped. "What is going on up there?"

"Rachel Deering doesn't feel very good," Dianne explained.

"Well, then go to the clinic, Rachel. I have a class to conduct."

Rachel fumbled with the clasp on her purse. Her hands were shaking wildly. *Don't let me pass out*, she begged silently. Finally she found her Life Savers and put three at once into her mouth. The entire room was staring at her now.

Slowly, as the candy dissolved, she began to feel better. And as her strength returned, her embarrassment grew.

"Are you all right now, Rachel?" Miss Hoggard asked at the next break.

"Yes," Rachel whispered, fighting to hold back her tears. She had never been so embarrassed in her life. The kids were whispering to each other.

"Then can we get back to the music?"

The pianist resumed the Christmas music. The basses managed to come in at the proper time. But Rachel sat very still in her chair . . . wishing she could die. Absolutely die.

All she wanted to do was go home. Home and away from her diabetes forever.

-SEVEN-

"**I** won't go! I'm telling you, I simply won't go!" Rachel slammed her bedroom door and threw herself across her bed.

"Open this door right now, young lady!" Her mother pounded on the door.

Rachel pulled her pillow over her head, wishing her mother would go away. But, of course, she didn't.

"I mean it, Rachel. Right now!"

Slowly she got up, walked over, and opened the door. Her mother stormed inside the room. "What's the meaning of this tantrum of yours?" she demanded.

"I told you," Rachel fumed, "I don't want to go!"

"Well, I'm telling you, you *are* going. Your sister has been chosen to dance in Madame Pershoff's Christmas concert, and we—and that includes *you*—are all going to watch her."

How could her parents be so unfair? Didn't they realize how hard it would be for her to go and sit there? To sit and watch all her friends dance? To watch Melanie dancing the part she had wanted so desperately? Why did Madame have to choose her dumb sister for the part in the concert anyway?

"Listen, Rachel," her mother continued, "you're the one who decided to quit dancing. Dr. Malar, your family, Madame Pershoff—all of us encouraged you to take it up again. But no. You took a little barre work three weeks ago and then walked out. No explanations. No nothing."

How could she tell them about her fear of insulin reactions? Ever since that day at school, Rachel had lived in fear of reactions. That day three weeks ago she had felt another one coming on at the barre and had run out of the studio and gotten a Coke just in time. Dr. Malar said reactions were just part of a diabetic's life. How could she dance, living in fear of passing out in class or on stage?

"I plan to go back to class," Rachel said defensively. "Right after the holidays. But I'm still trying to adjust—"

"Rachel, your father and I are very sorry about your diabetes. But we can't change it. Don't you think I'd trade places with you if I could?"

She looked at her mother. She could see that her mom really meant it!

"Now, I know how miserable it is to have your life turned upside down," Mrs. Deering said. "But it's time to start living again. After all, you're only thirteen. You can't crawl in a hole and disappear."

Rachel wished she could. She could think of nothing to say back to her mother.

"That nice McLaughlin boy says their group would love to have you visit and meet with them. Why don't you?"

"Because I don't want to be around a bunch of sick people!" she shot back. "And stop telling me about the Great Shawn McLaughlin. I'm sick of hearing about him!"

Her mother stiffened. "Suit yourself. But you're making a silly mistake. Everyone needs help at one time or another. Now get dressed. The concert starts in an hour and we are all going. I won't have your selfishness interfere with your sister's big evening." Then she left the room.

The old Olympus Theater was beautiful. Rachel thought of it as being left over from another era. The building was adorned with graceful curves and decorative stonework. Inside was plush pile carpeting in deep ruby red, thickly padded theater seats, and an enormous red velvet curtain. Rachel thought it was absolutely beautiful. And that night it was crowded with more than three hundred people.

Parents, families, and friends had come to watch Madame Pershoff's best ballet students perform. The people laughed, talked, and chattered in the crowded lobby, and then proceeded down the aisles to their seats. Everyone was eager to see the talented young dancers perform.

Rachel sat rigidly in her seat. She stared ahead at the huge curtain, hearing the sounds around her, yet knowing what it was like backstage. She imagined wild activity as dancers stretched, tied on pointe shoes, and preened in front of the makeup mirrors. And Madame would be hobbling around, tapping her silver-headed cane to the frantic pace. Rachel thought of the lovely costumes—with feathers, lace, sequins, and colors like a kaleidoscope. There would be last-minute problems to be fixed and tears of anticipation and stage fright. It was all happening back there—and Rachel sat out front. Cut off. Out of it. In another world. It was more than she could bear.

Then she saw him. Brandon Mitchell. He was standing close to the aisle, about five rows in front of her. And her agony was complete. Naturally he was there to watch Melanie in her triumphant moment as the Dying Swan. *I'm the one who's dying,* she thought. *Melanie has it all—Brandon and the part.*

The concert was beautiful. The dancers were talented, and their performances were excellent. The music was intoxicating. Chris did her little part as well as could be expected, Rachel thought. But by the time the finale came, and with it, the Dying Swan solo, Rachel's stomach was in knots.

Melanie's performance was flawless, so smooth and well done. Yet Rachel couldn't help but think how she would have interpreted the role, how she would have moved to the soulful music. She would have danced it differently. When the curtain came down and the audience cheered, Rachel knew that she could have danced it better. That was something for her to hold onto.

"Come on," her mother urged. "We're going backstage to get Chris."

"Do I have to?"

"Yes, you know what a madhouse it will be. I don't want her getting lost in the shuffle."

So Rachel ended up backstage after all, amid the excited squeals and the shouts of "It's over . . . and I didn't throw up!" She heard the laughter and sighs of exhaustion and watched dancers scurrying everywhere. Parents with cameras followed after little girls, big girls, and boys in colorful costumes and stage makeup.

"Here I am, Mom," Chris called excitedly. "Did you see me? Did I do all right?"

"Yes, you did, honey," Mrs. Deering announced, giving Chris a big hug. "Didn't you think so, Rachel?"

"Oh, yes. Fine." She could see Melanie standing in the center of a cluster of people. There were all congratulating her. Brandon smiled broadly. And Madame Pershoff nodded her approval. An unfamiliar man was standing at Madame's side.

"Rachel! Mrs. Deering!" Madame Pershoff's voice cut through the backstage noises. Rachel wished she could hide. But it was too late. Madame and the tall gentleman came toward them. Rachel could tell by the way he carried himself that he was a dancer.

"Rachel, I want you to meet Michael Tolavitch. We once danced together in Europe. Now Michael is with the New York City Ballet as an instructor and choreographer."

He was quite tall, with a mane of snow-white hair. He had dark blue eyes and the unmistakable grace and form of a dancer's discipline.

"So pleased to meet you." He nodded graciously while giving Rachel a penetrating look. "Tasha tells me that you've been ill, Rachel. A pity. She speaks highly of your talent. I wish I could have seen you dance tonight."

Rachel blushed. "Thank you."

• He scrutinized her carefully. "Yes, I can tell that you must have great form on the dance floor. Your head—it sets well. Your carriage is very good. And your height! Perfect. You know, we like a girl in our company to be at last five-foot-six or seven. Perhaps you will grow even taller."

Rachel could hardly believe her ears. Praise for her from a man like this! If only she could have danced for him . . .

"I will be returning in the late spring, Rachel. Perhaps you will be well enough to dance for me then?" He smiled.

"Maybe," she said and nodded.

Then he turned and walked away. But Madame lingered. She clasped Rachel's hands and said, "I knew he would like you. He has an instinct for talent. Rachel, he will be returning in May for the southeast regional auditions. I know they have several scholarships available for promising young ballerinas. And I would like so much to take you and Melanie and Patricia to the auditions. But you must get back into classes as soon as possible if you're to be ready for them. Think of it! A full scholarship to study all summer with the School of American Ballet of the New York City Ballet! Isn't it worth the work?"

Rachel was speechless, her head spinning with the excitement of the suggestion. "Once you told me," continued Madame Pershoff, "that you wanted to be a ballerina— 'more than anything!' Is that still the truth?"

She had so much to think about. Rachel sat in her living room and watched the Christmas tree lights twinkle and glow. A dance scholarship! It was every dancer's dream. There was a time when she'd have moved heaven and earth to go to the regional auditions for a company like the New York City Ballet.

But now? Now she had diabetes. Now she was afraid. *Why did this have to happen to me?* she thought with disgust. *If only I was well again. If only there were no more shots and special diets and testing. And no more insulin reactions.*

"What are you doing in the dark?" Her sister padded across the carpet and sat down on the floor in front of her.

"Wishing my fairy godmother would come along," Rachel said. Then she added, "I'd really like to be alone."

Chris ignored her request. "Wasn't tonight exciting, Rachel? I mean, to be asked by someone like Mr. Tolavitch to come to regional auditions. I hope I get asked someday."

"Sure. It was great."

"Aren't you going to do it?" Chris asked, wide-eyed.

"I'm not sure. I mean this diabetes thing—"

"Oh, good grief! People get diabetes every day."

"What do you know about it, smarty?" Rachel was angry.

"I know that you haven't been fit to live with since you came home from the hospital."

"Well, it didn't happen to you—"

"So what? I'm sorry you have to get shots every day and I don't. Does that make you feel better?"

"Oh, just shut up and go away." Tears sprang to Rachel's eyes.

"You bet I'll go away." Chris stood up. She was starting to cry, too. "But you want to know something? You're nothing but a big fat coward! You're just a quitter! You hear? A quitter!" And she ran from the room.

Rachel sat for a long time, watching the Christmas tree lights through her tears.

-EIGHT-

The Saturday after Christmas, Rachel was showing Jenny her presents when Shawn called. He told Rachel he had a soccer game later that day.

"So I just wondered if you'd like to come along to the game and watch me play," he asked.

Rachel turned to Jenny and whispered what he'd said.

"Go on!" Jenny mouthed.

"I don't know, Shawn—"

"Then after the game we'll stop by McDonald's and have some lunch. My treat," he added, laughing.

Jenny made a big face at her and dropped to the floor in a pretend faint.

"Okay, Shawn. What time?"

"Let's see . . . it's nine o'clock now and the game's at eleven. How about my dad and I pick you up about ten?"

"Sure. That will be fine. See you then." Rachel turned off the phone and said, "All right, Jen, you can cut it out. I'm going."

"I should hope so!" Jenny exclaimed. "I watched him at the game at school. He's a terrific player. Cute, too."

Rachel went into the kitchen to tell her mother, who nodded her surprised approval, and then went to her bedroom to get dressed. Jenny picked up the new Christmas skates she'd been showing Rachel and followed along.

"So, what do you wear to a soccer game?"

"Jeans," Jenny answered. "And it's kind of cool today. How about that baby-pink sweater of yours?"

Rachel pulled it out of her closet and put it on. She brushed her shiny brown hair and slipped a pink headband on to keep it out of her eyes. She put some blush on her cheeks, added some lip gloss, and looked at herself approvingly in the mirror.

"You look terrific," Jenny confirmed.

In spite of the way she felt about Shawn sometimes, Rachel was really pretty excited. It was a date. And the first *real* date she'd ever had. She'd always been too occupied with ballet and school to think much about dating anyway. Except for dreaming about Brandon Mitchell.

Funny, with the dance concert and Christmas vacation and everything, she hadn't thought about him once—until now. "Maybe I'd better eat a snack before I go," Rachel told Jenny. She didn't want to have a reaction today. "How long does a soccer game last anyway?"

They rode to the field quietly in the back seat of the car. Mr. McLaughlin didn't seem to notice they were back there, but Rachel felt self-conscious.

"The game'll last about an hour if there's no overtime. Then we'll hit McDonald's. I'm glad you decided to come," Shawn said.

She looked up at him shyly. He looked really cute. His uniform was a long-sleeved yellow jersey with a bold black stripe over one shoulder. The shorts, socks, and soccer shoes were black. He also wore black wristbands.

At the field, Rachel climbed up on the bleachers along with a small number of spectators. Even though the sun was shining, it was a colder-than-normal December day in Miami.

She watched the team do stretching exercises and noticed that many were the same kind of exercises that dancers did! She watched the boys kick the ball into the goal net. Shawn seemed very good. He slipped the ball past the goalie every time. By the time the whistle blew for the game to start, Rachel was impressed with Shawn's skills.

She became even more impressed as the game went on. Several times Shawn got the ball and raced up the side of the field, dribbling it all the way. He dodged his opponents artfully, sometimes passing the ball to a teammate, sometimes shooting the ball at the goal. Late in the first half, he scored. The people watching cheered. And so did Rachel. Suddenly she felt very proud to be the date of an athlete like Shawn.

And she noticed something else, too. The game of soccer was strenuous. Almost a full hour of non-stop running. No time-outs, except for injuries. And Shawn played every minute of the game. He ran as much as any of them. And he never once had an insulin reaction. By the time the game was over and Shawn's team had won it 3–0, Rachel was very curious and very excited.

"I'll have a double cheeseburger, a vanilla shake, and French fries," Shawn told the girl behind the service counter.

"I'll have the same," Rachel said.

"Hey," Shawn said, "I'm the one who played a soccer game. You'd better have a Diet Coke."

Rachel's cheeks burned. She'd forgotten. How rude of him to remind her in front of everybody.

They sat down and she stared out the window. "Mad at me?" he asked, unwrapping his burger.

"Of course not."

"Yeah, you are," he stated. "I know it's a drag having diabetes sometimes. I don't eat this way often. But I really poured it out in the game today. Dr. Malar doesn't see anything wrong with eating like this every once in a while."

She smiled at him and began to eat her lunch. "You know so much more about it than I do," she said, half to herself.

"I've had it longer."

"You know," she began haltingly, "you exercise hard in a game, but you don't seem to be afraid. I mean, don't you ever have insulin reactions?"

"Nope," he said flatly.

Rachel looked surprised.

"That's because I plan for it. When I know I've got a game or even practice, I eat extra carbohydrates. And I always have Gatorade at the field."

She looked at him skeptically. It seemed too simple.

"Rachel, I decided a long time ago that I was going to control my diabetes—it wasn't going to control me. Sure, it's a hassle—the shots, the diet. But I won't let it tell me what I can and can't do."

"And you think I let it control me?" she asked defensively.

"Are you still taking dance classes?"

"I'm going to start back right after Christmas break. When school starts again."

"Are you?" His look was penetrating and made her uncomfortable.

"Yes, I am!"

"Why don't you come to a diabetes meeting with me?" he asked, changing the subject. "You'll meet some great kids. Honest. We *all* have diabetes. We *all* have played little games with ourselves. Like juggling insulin so we can pig out on pizza. Skipping shots if it's not convenient to give them. Being scared a reaction will hit at the wrong time and place."

Her eyes met his squarely. He knew! He knew her greatest fear. And he wasn't laughing at her about it. He really did understand. A flood of relief swept over her.

"I—I don't know . . ."

"Come on." His hand touched hers. "We're getting together tomorrow afternoon at the bowling alley. It'll be fun. Then we'll all be going back to Molly Levine's house for pizza." Shawn leaned closer, his eyes twinkling. "And the proper assortment of fresh fruit on every diabetic's diet."

She laughed out loud. "Okay. I'll come. What time are you going to the bowling alley?"

"I'll pick you up at three o'clock—just in case you try and change your mind."

He might have been a whiz in soccer cleats, but in bowling shoes, Shawn was a real klutz. Rachel laughed so hard watching him that she got the hiccups. But he had been right about one thing—she was having fun.

The kids in the group were between twelve and sixteen years old. They were just plain, normal kids who all had one thing in common—diabetes. Some were outgoing while others were on the shy side, but they talked and acted just like all the other kids Rachel knew.

She like the adults who came along, the Levines, the McLaughlins, and Mrs. Swartz. Everybody bowled at least one game, and Rachel was glad that she didn't look too stupid.

But Shawn—he was a different story. He just couldn't get the hang of it. It didn't take her long to realize that he was the most popular one of the group, and that more than one girl was looking at her with real envy. She was very glad she had come.

Back at the Levines' home, they all sat around and ate and talked and shared their problems.

"Just once, I'd like to gorge on a hot fudge sundae—and *not* feel guilty," said a girl named Lori.

"Guilt didn't stop you from pigging out, though," someone teased.

"Diabetics cannot live on fruit alone!" she joked back. Everybody laughed.

"And I hate these gross lumps under my skin from giving myself shots all these years," said another girl.

Rachel looked at her, surprised.

"It's atrophy," Shawn explained in her ear. "Fatty layers start building up under your muscles after a while."

"Great," she said.

"And if my kid brother doesn't stop hiding Twinkies in our bedroom, I'll scream," said another.

"Aren't non-diabetic brothers and sisters the worst?"

And on and on it went. Rachel heard more about living with diabetes that afternoon than she had in the entire time she'd had the disease. It was good to have it out in the open, to talk about it and hear other kids' fears and problems. She was glad she'd come. Rachel was very glad Shawn hadn't given up on her.

She watched him out of the corner of her eye. He was not only cute, but he was smart and funny and very, very nice. She felt ashamed of the way she'd treated him before. Rachel knew that she wanted to see a lot more of him.

Rachel climbed the familiar stairs and peered inside the huge rehearsal studio. Afternoon sunlight streamed in from the high, overhead windows and bounced off the banks of mirrors.

"One and two . . . yes, yes, dancers. Lead with your heels." Madame Pershoff gave instructions from her straight-backed chair while Miss Lucy played the piano. "Now, *glissade devant* and *pas de chat* . . . again! Good!"

Rachel paused and watched the class work out. She was ready. More than anything, she wanted to get back to work.

"So you are ready to dance again?" Madame asked her after the class had left.

"Yes," Rachel said. "I want to be ready for those southeast regional auditions for the New York City Ballet."

Madame gazed at her hard. "You have been out a long time, Rachel. Almost three months. It will be very hard to get back into shape. Are you willing to work harder than ever before in your life?"

"Yes, I am." And she meant it.

"Good," Madame said and nodded, "because I want to take you to those auditions. I think you can be a very fine dancer."

-NINE-

Madame Pershoff was right. Rachel never worked harder in her life. Every day after school for two hours or more, four hours on Saturdays, practice and rehearsal, special exercises at home. Her muscles ached, at first so badly that she could hardly limp around school. And at night, she was so exhausted that she fell into bed the minute she finished her homework.

Her days became a ritual of routine. Up at six for stretching exercises. Breakfast and insulin shot. School. Dance class from three to five. Dinner and insulin shot. Homework and bed. On evenings when she had no homework, she went back to the studio for more classes.

Sunday was her only "day off." After church she messed around with Jenny. Every other Sunday, she attended the diabetes youth group meeting where she saw Shawn. Rachel looked forward to being with him. But his schedule was busy, too. He had soccer practice often and games every Saturday. Sometimes they talked on the phone, but mostly they were very involved with their own activities.

Rachel's goal was to be ready for the May auditions. So she planned her life around that goal and her diabetes. She learned to eat extra food before class to avoid reactions. She took excellent care of herself. Nothing was going to interfere with those auditions . . . not school, not friends, not even her diabetes.

She noticed that Melanie was working just as hard. She wanted a scholarship, too. Well, maybe there'd be scholarships for both of them. But if there wasn't, then Rachel was going to be sure that she got one.

"Ah come on, Rachel. Just ask him. We can all go together. It'll be fun," Jenny pleaded with Rachel between bites of lunch in the cafeteria.

"I don't know. I mean, I've never asked a boy anywhere," Rachel said, shaking her head.

"So, there's always a first time. And I'll bet you he'd love to come."

Rachel pushed the food around on her tray. Her heart was pounding with anticipation. The Valentine's Dance. Everyone in the school was talking about it, and everybody who was anybody was going to it. The dance committee had been working on decorations and refreshments for weeks. It would be fun to go.

"Rachel, think about it," Jenny continued. "Me and Ben and you and Shawn. Mr. Cole already said he'd drive us. Come on. Ask him."

Later that night Rachel talked to her parents about it. The Deerings exchanged glances. "Well, honey, if you'd really like to go with Shawn, then ask him," her dad advised.

"Sure," her mother agreed. "We can invite the McLaughlins over to play cards that night and you and Shawn can go with Jenny and Ben. Then when you get back here, his parents can take him on home. I'm sure you'll have fun."

"But I don't have anything to wear . . . ," Rachel's voice trailed off.

"No woman ever does," her father said with a smile. "Why don't you and Mom go shopping next Saturday?"

Rachel started to protest, "But I have ballet—"

"After class," he assured her. "I am sure you can find *something* between the hours of one and nine!"

"Could we, Mom?" Rachel asked, her excitement growing. She *did* want to go to that dance.

"Of course, we can," her mother answered. "But don't you think you'd better ask Shawn first?"

"Oh, sure." Her heart was pounding. "Maybe I'll call him right now."

Rachel picked up the phone nearby. Her hand started shaking. *Stop it,* she told herself. *For heaven's sake, it's only Shawn. We've been to lots of things together.* But she couldn't shake her nervousness.

It was scary to pick up a phone and ask someone for a date. *How did boys get the guts?* She wondered. *What if he said 'no'? Worse yet, what if he laughs at me? "Go out with you? To your school's stupid dance? I'm busy."* She shook her head and tried to clear away the negative thoughts.

Rachel took a deep breath and pushed the numbers for Shawn's house. "Darn!" she said aloud. Her finger had slipped off the last button and she'd misdialed. Angrily she hung up.

Suddenly, Rachel heard a giggle. She looked around. No one. Then she heard it again.

"Chris!" she shouted. Sure enough. There sat her sister, crouching behind the door, holding her hand over her mouth, and trying hard not to laugh. "You get lost, you little brat!"

Chris stuck out her tongue at Rachel. Rachel took a swing, but missed.

"Mother!" Chris yelped, ducking the swat. "Rachel hit me!"

"I did not! But she's listening in on my conversation—"

"Girls!" Mrs. Deering came down the hall and grabbed them both. "You two stop that this instant! Now, Chris, go to your room. This is Rachel's private call and you have no business listening in."

"Oh, all right." Chris shuffled toward her room. "But he'll probably say no. Who'd want to go to a dance with *her?*"

"Chris! You stop it!"

But the damage was done. Rachel's last bit of self-confidence evaporated. "See what I mean?" Rachel wailed to her mother. "She's such a brat."

"That will do. Look, if you want to ask Shawn to the dance, do it. But stop prolonging the agony. The worst that can happen is that he can't go." Her mom left the hallway and Rachel turned back to the phone.

"A lot she knows," Rachel grumbled. But she picked up the receiver again. This time she dialed the number correctly.

It rang four times before a voice answered. "Hello, McLaughlins' residence." It was Mrs. McLaughlin. Rachel's heart was pounding.

"M–may I speak to Shawn?" She sure wished her voice sounded more secure.

"Just a minute. I'll get him."

It seemed like an eternity before she heard his voice. "Hello?"

"Hi, Shawn? It's me . . . Rachel."

"Oh, hi."

He doesn't sound too excited about hearing from me, she thought. She paused, and there was a long, awkward silence. "Whatcha doing?" she asked.

"Homework." More dead silence.

"Um . . . I was wondering if maybe you'd like to . . . I mean, my school is having a Valentine's dance next Saturday . . . that is, a week from next Saturday . . . Well, what I'd like to know is if maybe you'd like to come with me . . . and my friends Ben and Jenny." There! She'd said it.

"Say that again?" he asked.

"I want to know if you'd like to come to my school Valentine's dance a week from Saturday." Rachel felt exasperated. Why couldn't she be cool like Jenny? *I'll bet Jenny wouldn't have gotten all tongue-tied*, she thought.

"Sure," he said.

"What?" she asked.

"I said, 'sure,'" Shawn repeated.

"Well, super." Rachel felt relief wash over her. "My parents said something about inviting your folks over that night for cards. I guess Mom will be calling soon . . ." her voice trailed off. She couldn't think of much else to say. "We'll be riding with Jenny and Ben. His dad's driving . . ."

"Sounds good to me," Shawn said.

"Well . . . thanks. I'll talk to you about it more later."

She felt like an idiot. And she couldn't think of anything else to say. "Bye."

"Bye," he echoed. Then he added, "And thanks, Rachel."

She hung up the phone. She was weak and perspiring, but she felt proud. She'd asked him! And he said yes!

If Mom drags me into one more store, I'll scream! Rachel thought. They'd been shopping for three hours and couldn't agree on anything.

"Jeans!" Mrs. Deering had exclaimed. "You already own seven pairs. No way, young lady. You're not going to a dance in jeans!"

"But, Mom, everyone will be wearing jeans. I'll look dumb all dressed up. Besides, three pairs of my jeans are rags. I only wear them around the house. I want a new pair."

"Forget it, Rachel."

"But Mom . . ." And so it had gone. From store to store. Rachel dutifully tried on sweaters and skirts while she looked longingly at the jeans departments.

They were both tired when they entered a small boutique in the mall that catered to girls her age. A helpful saleslady sized up the situation immediately and offered her seasoned experience.

Rachel sulked as the woman showed her several pairs of dress pants. But she finally held up a pair that both Rachel and her mother liked. Rachel tried them on. They were flattering, low-rise wool pants in a gray herringbone pattern.

Next the saleslady showed them a fitted, V-neck sweater in a pale pink color. Finally, she coordinated everything with a pair of dangling, pink-beaded earrings. Rachel stared at herself in the dressing room mirror. She had to admit that she looked pretty pulled together.

Once the outfit was purchased, the tension between Rachel and her mother evaporated. They began to have fun together. Mrs. Deering took Rachel into the department store and bought her new pink blush, tinted lip-gloss, and a spray bottle of perfume. By the time they arrived home, they were beaming and content.

On the night of the dance, Rachel gazed at herself in the mirror in her room for a long time. Her clothes were stylish and perfect. Her make-up made her look very grown-up. And her short dark hair was curled back from her face after half an hour with her curling iron. All in all, she thought she looked better than she ever had looked before.

The look on Shawn's face when she walked into the room to leave for the dance told Rachel that he thought so, too.

-TEN-

"Would you look at this place!" Jenny exclaimed. "What a crowd scene."

The cafeteria was jammed with kids. Rachel stood holding Shawn's hand at the doorway and wondered how the four of them would ever squeeze in the place.

Music from the DJ set up on the stage blasted out into the cool night air. Red and white hearts hung on the walls along with yards of matching crepe paper streamers. Along one wall there were rows of chairs and along another, long tables piled high with Cokes, chips, and pretzels.

Rachel recognized several teachers standing around acting as chaperones. Most didn't appear to be having much fun, except for Mr. Perez. It was easy to see why the PE coach was the most popular teacher in the school. He really fit in with the kids and sometimes seemed like one of them.

The four of them squeezed into the cafeteria and immediately found themselves shouting above the din. "Let's go up and watch the DJ for a minute!" Ben suggested. Shawn held Rachel's hand firmly and wove a path through the dancing couples.

Together they stood and watched the DJ go through his routine. In between songs he kept up a line of chatter into his mike. "Let's do something a little bit slower now, fans . . ."

Instantly, the music shifted to a slow and softer beat. All around them, dancers fused together. Shawn turned to Rachel and gently pulled her closer. Suddenly she felt very shy. *Stop it!* she told herself. *This is Shawn. Why should I feel this way around him?* But as he took her in his arms and pulled her closer, her heart started pounding.

He smelled fresh and minty, and his wool sweater felt scratchy against her cheek. It was good to be so near him. His hands were warm and reassuring. "You know," he said into her ear, "I was kind of scared to come here with you."

She pulled back and looked into his sparkling blue eyes. "Scared? Why?"

"Do you know what it's like to go to a dance with a REAL dancer?"

"Oh, you're so silly," she smiled.

"No, I mean it," he teased. "What if I dance like I bowl? You took a real chance."

Rachel laughed out loud remembering the bowling party. "You're right. But I'm glad I took the chance. Besides, I don't do this kind of dancing in ballet and you know it."

"I'd like to see you dance sometime. How about those auditions you've been training so hard for? Could I come to them?"

"Are you kidding?" Rachel laughed. "Parents aren't even allowed to come. No, Madame Pershoff will pick us up in the morning of the audition and take us to the studio where they're being held. Then we'll fill out cards, get a number, and stand around being nervous till we're called. Sometimes the judges just take one look at you and disqualify you."

"What? Without even giving you a chance?"

"Well, ballerinas have to look a special way. And if you don't have that look, then so long."

"Well, you look fine to me," he added.

"I hope I look fine to them," she smiled.

They danced on and on, from slow dances to fast ones. Everything the DJ played, they danced to. Rachel hardly had time to catch her breath before another song started playing. She was having the best time of her whole life. She realized with a start that she adored Shawn McLaughlin. It was wonderful to have him so close to her. To have him hold her.

Rachel also decided that her mother had been right. Her dress pants were perfect for the dance. Sure, a lot of kids wore jeans. But a lot were dressed like her, too.

Shawn looked particularly handsome to her. He wore jeans and a camel-colored sweater that set off his copper-colored hair. Rachel noticed more than one girl looking at her enviously. She even overheard Sally Andrews ask Cindy Curtis, "Who's that with Rachel? He's something else. Is he her boyfriend?"

A boyfriend! Rachel thought with a start. But yes, that's exactly who Shawn was . . . Rachel's boyfriend. He'd been a friend to her. A real friend. And now . . . he was beginning to mean even more.

"I have an idea," Shawn interrupted her thoughts. "Why don't we sit one out and let me get us a couple of Cokes. We deserve the 'real thing.'" He winked at her and she caught his meaning instantly. Two diabetics needing a shot of sugar. She laughed out loud at his clever choice of words.

He guided her over to a chair and she sat down gratefully. She was thirsty. Rachel watched him ease into the crowd and head toward the refreshment table. She bent down to rub her foot.

"How about a dance, Rachel? Before your main man comes back?"

She looked up with a start at Brandon Mitchell.

"I–I don't . . . I mean . . . Where's Melanie?" Rachel was totally flustered.

"Out of sight, out of mind," he told her with a grin.

"I can't." She felt her cheeks flush. Where was Shawn? Why didn't he come back?

"Oh, come on," Brandon said, grabbing her hand and pulling her to her feet. "You look terrific! And I'll bet you'd really like to dance with me."

Rachel tried to pull away from him. The conceit! "No! Please, I don't want anything from you." She was on the verge of tears.

"Take your hands off her!" Shawn's voice cut through the air.

Brandon dropped her hand and she retreated to Shawn's side. "Hey," Brandon shrugged, "I just wanted Miss High-and-Mighty to dance."

Shawn glared at Brandon. He wasn't afraid of him at all.

"Brandon! I've been looking every place for you." Melanie slipped up beside Brandon and put her arm through his. She glanced anxiously from Brandon to Shawn to Rachel.

"I'm right here, Mel," Brandon said crossly. "Stop hanging on me." And he turned on his heel and left her standing there. Melanie looked stricken. She stared at Rachel, then turned and went after Brandon.

"Oh, Shawn, how could he do that to her? How embarrassing." For the first time ever, Rachel felt sorry for Melanie Hallick.

"The guy's a creep," Shawn said. "Here, drink your Coke."

Rachel sat and sipped the liquid in silence. How could she have been so blind to what Brandon Mitchell was really like? How could she have ever had a crush on him? She couldn't believe he could be so thoughtless and cruel.

The she looked gratefully at Shawn. *How lucky I am to have a boyfriend like you*, she thought. And she leaned over and took his hand. "Thank you," she said.

"What for? I should have punched his lights out."

"Do you fight better than you bowl?" she teased.

Rachel couldn't believe the dance was over. It seemed as if they'd just gotten there. But the lights had been turned up and the DJ was putting away his equipment. The four of them waited outside in the crisp night air for Ben's father.

"That was great!" Jenny chattered on and on. "Did you see Mary Bagley? Honestly, I think she found that outfit at Goodwill.

And how about you, Rachel? Almost the cause of a fight."

"Oh stop it!" Rachel told her, snuggling closer to Shawn. Just then, Mr. Cole arrived and they all slid into the car. Mercifully, they rode in silence to Rachel's house.

Shawn thanked Mr. Cole and they stood and watched as the car slipped off into the night. Shawn took Rachel's hand and they started up the winding walkway together.

"Do you think they heard the car?" she asked.

"Are you kidding? My mom has 20/20 hearing."

Rachel giggled. "That's eyesight, silly. But I know what you mean. My mother probably heard everything that went on at the dance."

They reached her front door. The porch light burned like a beacon and Rachel reached for the doorknob.

"Wait!" Shawn whispered, pulling back her hand.

She turned and looked up at him. "Don't go inside yet," he said.

"But it's worse than daylight out here," she said.

"Yes, I know." But he reached up and loosened two screws on the porch light fixture with a dime. Rachel watched, fascinated. The fixture dropped down, fastened to the wood by the two remaining screws.

"What are you doing?" she whispered.

"You'll see."

Then Shawn pulled his sleeve down over his hand and carefully turned the hot light bulb until it blinked off. Suddenly they were standing in the dark.

"Dad will be out like a shot," she warned.

"Maybe they've got a hot hand of cards going and won't notice," he said.

Just then, the moon broke through the cloud cover and blinked through the trees overhead. Shawn put both arms around Rachel and pulled her close. Her heart was pounding.

"Why did you do that?" she asked softly.

"How could I kiss you goodnight with all that light shining in my eyes?" he answered.

Then, very gently, Shawn pressed his lips against hers. They were very warm and very soft . . .

Rachel lay in bed awake. She watched the moonlight pour in through her half-raised blinds. She could still hear the music from the dance in her head. She could still feel Shawn's arms around her. *This was the greatest night in my life!* she thought happily.

She wished she could store this night away forever. What would become of her and Shawn? And all her plans to become a ballerina? She still wanted that. But she wanted to be with him, too.

Well, in three months she would compete in the auditions. Maybe she'd even win a scholarship to the School of American Ballet. It was all still very important to her. But she also knew that if she didn't win a scholarship this time, she would live through it. And she'd try again. All because of Shawn.

He'd made her realize that life was beautiful. And that even having diabetes wasn't going to stop her. Nothing could keep her from fulfilling her dreams.

-ELEVEN-

The lobby was a whirlwind of activity. Over 200 nervous would-be ballerinas paced, sat, stood, and lounged against the walls of the North Miami Dance Studio. Rachel could hardly believe her eyes.

Where had so many dancers come from? "As far away as Atlanta," Madame Pershoff had warned them in the car during the long ride over. "The competition will be very stiff."

Rachel believed her. Every dancer who had ever dreamed of a career in ballet wanted a scholarship to a leading ballet school. And the School of American Ballet of the New York City Ballet was one of the best.

Rachel was nervous. She and Pat and Melanie had ridden over with Madame in subdued silence. It had been raining. And now, amid all this confusion, Rachel's months and months of work might pay off for her.

She finished filling out the card the staff had given her. "Let's see," she said, reading it over quietly to herself. "Name, address, age, years in training, instructor, weight, height . . ." Yes, it all seemed to be there. She handed in the card and a woman handed her a number. 78. They would call 35 girls at a time. So that meant she'd be in the third group to go into the studio for the audition.

Darn! She had to go to the bathroom! Whenever she was nervous, her blood sugar got higher. And higher blood sugar meant more trips to the bathroom. *Well*, Rachel thought, *I've had my extra shot and my extra snack. I know I can make it through my audition without any problems.* She didn't want the judges to know about her diabetes. Not yet anyway. If she got a scholarship, then they could know. But she didn't want anything to count against her.

"You can do it." That's what Shawn had told her last night on the phone. She felt that she really could—then. But now, with all these girls trying for such a small number of scholarships . . .

"Ladies! Please. Numbers 71 through 106," a petite woman announced from the studio doors. Rachel caught her breath and glanced anxiously at Madame Pershoff. The white-haired woman nodded and smiled at her. Rachel took a deep breath and filed into the large studio. "Here goes my future," she whispered.

She stood there looking like a goddess. Rachel could hardly take her eyes off her. The chief judge for the auditions was one of the foremost ballerinas of the New York City Ballet. From the corner of her eye, Rachel could also see Michael Tolavitch, Madame Pershoff's friend from the Christmas concert.

The suspense was agonizing. All the contestants stood lined up at the barre while the judges stared at them. Rachel knew they were each being appraised and evaluated on body type. Some of the girls wouldn't make it past the test alone. They just wouldn't have the right look—the right shape or posture. And even so much as one extra ounce of fat meant instant dismissal.

Rachel stood very still. Her head was erect. Her back was straight. Her arms hung gracefully at her sides. *Why is she staring at me so hard?* Rachel felt the judge's eyes going over and over her. *Oh, please, God, don't let me lose it like this*, she prayed silently. The judge jotted notes on Rachel's card and then surveyed her again.

"Very well," the judge announced suddenly, "79, 90, 84, and 101—you may be excused."

. Number 90 burst into tears and fled the room. Rachel felt very sorry for her. But she breathed a deep sigh, grateful that she was allowed to progress to the barre work.

The piano music began and the judge called out various steps and directions. "Fifth position! And *battement battu* . . . and *battemont fondu* . . ." Rachel moved through the familiar steps with ease. How exciting! She was sure of herself now, so she danced in total confidence.

Again, the judge stared at her. Again, she marked the card. Muscle control . . . placement . . . turnout—Rachel knew that this was what she was being judged on. Mr. Tolavitch stopped in front of her. He appraised

Rachel carefully. Then he stepped over to the judge and said something.

I hope it's not a dismissal, Rachel thought. But her fear never showed in her dancing. She followed each direction carefully.

"Number 72, 75, 86 . . ." When she had finished, 12 more girls had been dismissed. Rachel surveyed the remaining dancers. Only 11 of them left. *At least I'm one of them*, she thought.

"Please move to the center floor," the judge directed. The girls obeyed quickly. "We will do half of center work in soft shoes, then we will switch to pointe," she announced.

The piano began and so did the exercises. Rachel knew that this was the place that her muscle control would really count. She was glad she'd always been a strong person. A flash of memory brought Shawn to her mind. He's strong, too. A diabetic soccer player. A diabetic ballerina. They could both beat their disease.

The small group advanced onto pointe. Rachel tied the new ribbons on her pointe shoes and went through the combinations. *They keep staring at me*, she thought. But she refused to let it upset her and throw off her performance. *I'm still in the running*, she told herself as she and the other girls danced across the floor.

"Thank you, ladies!" the judge announced.

It was over! Rachel breathed a sigh of relief.

"In about three or four weeks each of you will be notified by letter whether you have been awarded a full or partial scholarship, or you will be encouraged to try again. Your instructor and studio will also be notified of our decision. We would like to thank all for you for coming to today's auditions."

Rachel had been the last of Madame's students to audition. They all rode back home together in silence. Pat was red-eyed. She had been dismissed from her group after the barre work. So it came down to Rachel and Melanie. Again. It was possible that both of them could be offered scholarships—but unlikely. Or perhaps neither would win one.

Rachel glanced over at Melanie. Cool, calm, aloof. As if she'd just sat through a not too interesting movie. Ho-hum. *Well, I remember when she wasn't quite so composed*, Rachel thought sourly. That night Brandon made a fool out of her. Immediately Rachel felt ashamed of herself.

Nothing was ever going to change Melanie. And that was too bad from Rachel's viewpoint. Because being "perfect" all your life would be a very boring thing to be.

The first person she called about the auditions was Shawn.

"Well, I didn't get kicked off the floor!" she told him jokingly.

"Hey! They know talent when they see it," he reminded her. "When will you know something?"

"About a month. I don't think I can stand it."

"What if you win?"

"I'd go to New York for six weeks and take classes at the School of American Ballet with the New York City Ballet Company. And when you take classes there, you have a chance to be seen by some of the best Ballet Masters in the world!"

"I guess that would be like me studying with David Beckham," he said. "He's a great soccer star."

"Oh, who knows? We may both be famous yet."

The next person she called was Jenny, who talked nonstop until Rachel thought her ear would fall off.

"New York! Oh, I bet you get it, Rachel. I know you're the best there is."

"Thanks. But I was one of 200 trying out. Besides, even if I don't win this time, I'll go back next year."

That night at the dinner table, Rachel recounted every detail to her family. Even Chris listened, enthralled. Her parents didn't say too much. Just, "That's nice, dear." That was strange. She would have thought they'd have been more enthusiastic. After all, they'd wanted her to go back to dancing. Now they acted like they didn't care one way or the other if she got a scholarship. Parents were strange people sometimes!

The first two weeks dragged by. Rachel raced home from ballet every day and checked the mail. No letter from the School of American

Ballet. The story was the same the third week. By the start of the fourth week, she was depressed about it.

"Maybe it got lost in the mail," Chris suggested. But Rachel didn't think so. Shawn encouraged her every night on the phone. Madame Pershoff said nothing to her about it during classes. Wasn't she ever going to hear from them?

School began to wind down. Exams began. In only two more weeks, school would be out for the summer. Even though Rachel was making all A's and B's again, she didn't feel satisfied. "I can't stand this waiting!" she told Shawn angrily one night on the phone. "I think a rejection would be better than waiting like this."

"No it wouldn't," he said. And she knew he was right. So the days dragged by. School, dance class, a soccer match with Shawn . . . but no letter.

Rachel avoided both Melanie and Brandon like the plague. Besides, things were considerably cooler between Brandon and Melanie anyway. Brandon had developed a sudden interest in pretty Gail Lawler and pointedly ignored

Melanie at school. Naturally Melanie acted like it didn't matter one bit to her. But sometimes Rachel caught her staring at him across the cafeteria. *I'll bet she's dying inside*, Rachel often thought to herself.

Rachel shut her history book and flipped off her stereo. "There!" she said. "If I don't know it now, I never will." She heard the phone ringing. Her mother called, "Rachel! It's for you!"

"All right!" she called back.

"It's Madame Pershoff," Mrs. Deering said, handing Rachel the receiver. Rachel's heart began to pound.

"Y–yes?"

"I just got to my mail," the accented voice explained. "I got a letter today from the School of American Ballet." She paused and Rachel could hear her own breath.

"They only awarded five scholarships this time. Two full ones and three partials. I am very proud that one of the full scholarships went to one of my girls."

Sweat poured off Rachel's hands. The phone receiver was damp and slippery. "Melanie?" she asked breathlessly.

"Why no, my dear. They have offered it to you."

For a few seconds Rachel was speechless. Then she shouted, "I got it! You really mean it? They gave ME the scholarship?"

Madame Pershoff's voice danced as she confirmed the news. Rachel leaped up and down clutching the phone. "I can't believe it? It's wonderful! Me! Going to New York! Oh, Madame Pershoff! Thanks so much for calling!" She hung up. She had to find her mother.

She hurried down the hall toward the spacious kitchen. Her mother stood at the sink loading the dishwasher. "Mom! Guess what? Mom! I won! A full dance scholarship . . ." Rachel's voice trailed off. Her mother seemed to be ignoring her.

"Mom? Did you hear me? I said, 'I won.' Aren't you glad?"

Mrs. Deering turned around slowly. Her face contained a controlled smile. But Rachel could tell by the look in her eyes that something was wrong. "Of course I heard you. And naturally, I'm very pleased for you."

"Well, you don't act like it," Rachel accused. Fear suddenly clutched at her heart.

"It was very thoughtful of Madame Pershoff to call you, Rachel," Mrs. Deering said. "But I need to talk to you about it."

Rachel stood staring at her mother's face. It wasn't her imagination. Something was wrong. "I thought you'd be thrilled for me," Rachel began in a quiet voice. "They only gave out five scholarships. And I got one."

"Rachel," her mom began, taking her by her shoulders, "I *am* happy for you. I know that you've received a great honor. But I'm sorry, honey. You absolutely, positively cannot go."

-TWELVE-

Rachel recoiled as if she'd been slapped. All the color drained from her face. "What?" she whispered in disbelief.

"Your father and I discussed it at great length. We talked a long time about what we'd do if you won. We can't send you off to New York—"

"But why?" Rachel moaned, tears starting down her cheeks.

"How can we let you go to a strange city?"

"But the school's set up to help students get adjusted. They help you get an apartment. They help you—"

"Rachel," Mrs. Deering interrupted. "You're not going and that's final."

Suddenly, a nagging thought hit Rachel hard. "It's because of my diabetes, isn't it?" she asked between sobs.

Her mom said nothing, but Rachel could tell she'd discovered the truth. "You're afraid I won't take care of myself. But I will! I promise, I will!"

"No, that's not it . . ."

But Rachel knew that she was right. It was her diabetes.

"Honey," Mrs. Deering tried to reason, "you've done a wonderful job handling your diabetes. You take excellent care of yourself. But think about it. You'd be over 1500 miles away from home. Away from your doctor, your friends, your family. I plan all your meals and cook them. I know just what you need—and when you need it. And what if you got sick? What if your blood sugar went out of control? How would you manage?"

Suddenly Rachel was angry. "All along, you've nagged at me to keep dancing. You kept after me to accept my illness and to go on with ballet classes in spite of it."

"Yes, and we still want you to. Dancing is so good for your diabetic control—"

"But what about me?" Rachel burst out. "I want to dance for ME—not for my control! Don't you see? I want to be a professional dancer!"

"And you still can, honey. But later. After you've had more time to adjust. Why, you can get another scholarship next year—"

"Next year!" Rachel exploded. "But they're offering it to me now! I can't wait a whole year. They want me now. And if I'm good enough for them this summer, they could ask me back next year to dance in the ballet corps. But I've got to go right now."

"I'm sorry, Rachel. But it's out of the question. Your father and I can't let you go. We can't take the chance. Something might happen to you."

"Please!" Rachel sobbed. "Why won't you trust me? I'll be fine, I know it."

"I won't discuss it any more. Your dad's working late, but when he comes home, he'll come talk to you. Maybe he can explain it better."

"I'll NEVER forgive you if you don't let me go! You'll ruin my whole life!"

Rachel ran from the kitchen in tears. She made it to the safety of her bedroom and flung herself across the bed. And she cried and cried . . . as if her heart were breaking . . .

Rachel stayed in her darkened room for over an hour. Her eyes were red and swollen. She felt all cried out. It just wasn't fair! How could her parents do this to her? After all her hard work and all her dreams . . .

Shawn! She'd call him. He'd help her. With shaking fingers, she dialed his number. But the minute she heard his voice, a huge lump rose in her throat, and she could barely speak.

"Rachel?" he asked. "Is that you?"

"Y–yes," she mumbled.

"What's wrong?" He sounded concerned.

Numbly, she told him the whole story. Yes, she'd gotten the scholarship. But her parents refused to let her take it. They were afraid. Afraid of her diabetes. Afraid to let her be on her own.

"It's a bummer," he said. "I don't know what to say. Listen, why don't you call Dr. Malar? Maybe he can get them to change their minds."

"I don't think it will help. They won't give in," said Rachel sadly.

"Give it a try, Rachel. It can't hurt. I know he'd like to hear about it anyway."

"Well, maybe," she said softly. Dr. Malar had told her to call him whenever she needed him. Well, she sure needed him now.

"Thanks, Shawn," she whispered and hung up.

She'd never called a doctor before. Her parents had always taken care of those things for her. But she looked up his number and dialed it. His answering service picked up the call.

"May I help you?"

"This—this is Rachel Deering. I need to speak to Dr. Malar."

"Is this an emergency?"

"No. I mean, yes. I just have to talk to him! I'm one of his patients."

"Could you tell me the nature of your problem?" The woman sounded impatient.

She felt like saying, "I'm dying!" But instead she said, "I must talk to him right away—about a problem with my diabetes." There! That got some results.

"I'll have him call you. What's your number?"

Rachel told her and then waited by the phone. She had to get it on the first ring. She didn't want her mother picking up the phone.

The phone gave a short ring and Rachel grabbed it.

"Hello," she whispered.

"Rachel?" It was Malar's voice.

"Oh, Dr. Malar. Please help me."

The four of them sat looking at each other. Dr. Malar leaned in his office chair, his hands locked behind his head. He was listening intently to Mr. Deering. Rachel's mother sat straight upright, twisting her rings on her fingers. Rachel stared hard at Dr. Malar's diploma on his office wall, wishing the afternoon were over.

"So, you see," her father finished, "while we're very proud of Rachel's achievement, we just can't send her off for six weeks."

"Well," Dr. Malar began, his blue eyes filled with concern. "New York is not exactly the backwoods of America. I personally know several well-qualified doctors there. I'd feel confident in calling any of them to handle Rachel's case temporarily."

Rachel's heart leaped up with renewed hope.

"It's not just the medical reasons—" Mrs. Deering started.

"I know," Dr Malar interrupted. "But let's face it, if it weren't for the diabetes, would you be having the same doubts?"

Neither one of her parents would answer him. "Look," he continued, "Rachel's come a long way since her diagnosis. She went through very typical behavior patterns. First, disbelief. Then anger . . . frustration . . . rejection. She even tried to drop out of life over it."

Rachel blushed, remembering how mean she'd been to everyone at the beginning.

"But she came to grips with it. She got back into dancing, even joined our diabetic youth group. Her control is very good. Her blood sugar readings are acceptable. Her diabetes is no reason to keep her home."

"Yes, but there's so much responsibility on her," her mother said.

"That's true. And there always will be. She's got to take care of herself for the rest of her life. And the quality of that care will determine the quality of her life. Don't base your decision on her disease. There are many doctors who can help Rachel in New York. Make your decision on what's best for Rachel. She's a bright, mature girl. And most important, she's not afraid. And that's the most important step of all."

Rachel watched her parents' faces. She saw their confusion. That gave her hope. But she also sensed their determination not to let her go. That filled her heart with fear. Didn't they know they were deciding her whole future?

Rachel had never in her entire life listened in on her parents' private conversations. But she just couldn't help herself now. They were sitting in the kitchen. Her parents and Mrs. McLaughlin.

Shawn had told Rachel his mother was coming over to talk to her mom and dad. And Rachel was glad. Her parents hadn't changed their minds yet, but they were beginning to see her side.

Rachel sat down in the hallway outside the kitchen and listened intently to the conversation.

"I know just how you feel," Mrs. McLaughlin said after Rachel's mom finished talking. "I'll never forget the first time Shawn's soccer team went away on an overnighter. He was ten years old. They had a big championship match in Jacksonville. The whole team was supposed to drive up, spend the night, and get to the field early the next morning. Well, I just couldn't face the thought of him 'managing' without me. So, I went along. There were 16 little soccer players, four coaches . . . and me. I know that Shawn was embarrassed to death."

"Yes, but that was just for one night," Mrs. Deering protested. "They want Rachel for six weeks."

"Then the next time," Mrs. McLaughlin continued, "they went to play in a tournament in Washington, D.C. I just knew he couldn't make it without me. So I went then, too. And I'm glad I did. It gave me a confidence about him I could never have gotten otherwise. He did fine. In fact, he's done fine every time. I stopped going along two years ago. He doesn't need me. He manages his diabetes just fine. Why, his coach is talking about taking the team to England next summer." Marge laughed out loud.

"But that's one trip I'm going on. Not because Shawn needs me . . . but because *I* want to go to England. Why should he have all the fun?"

Rachel wished she could hug Shawn's mother. She could tell that her parents were becoming less scared.

"I don't know . . . ," Mrs. Deering said.

"Go with her," Shawn's mother urged.

"What?"

"Go with her. Get her settled in. Contact the doctors yourself. Stay a few days—even a week—and then come home. You won't feel like you're sending her off into the unknown that way. And she'll feel better about it, too. As much as she's begging you to let her go, I know she's scared a little, too. She needs you to have confidence in her in order for her to feel really good about going.

"I hope you'll change your minds. This is more than just a dance scholarship. For Rachel, it's a pattern for the rest of her life. She can let her diabetes control her life—or she can control her life herself."

Rachel sat clutching Shawn's hand tightly. The hustle and activity of the airport was all around them. Flight numbers were called. Passengers hurried past. Her father waited patiently in line to check their baggage. Fortunately, her mother had taken Chris to the bathroom so Rachel and Shawn were by themselves.

"I'm going to miss you," Shawn said.

Rachel felt a lump in her throat. "I'll miss you, too. I'll write every day."

"You'd better dance every day," he teased. "Besides, it's only six weeks. I'll be here to meet your plane when it lands."

"Promise?"

"I promise." He glanced around, then leaned over and kissed her lightly.

She *was* going to miss him. And the kids in the diabetic youth group. And Jenny.

"I heard them call your plane!" Chris announced, running up to them. Shawn pulled

Rachel up beside him, and together they started toward the departure gates. Her mother and father walked quickly ahead, but Chris lingered alongside of them. She kept staring at Shawn, open admiration in her little girl eyes.

"Go on up with Mom," Rachel urged her.

"I want to walk with you," Chris said stubbornly.

"Go on! Shoo!"

Tears welled up in Chris's eyes. "I'll miss you," she mumbled.

Rachel stopped and bent over her sister. She felt like crying a little, too. "No, you won't. Listen. If you promise to take extra good care of them, I'll let you use my CDs until I get home."

"You will?" Chris' face beamed. "Mom! Dad! Guess what!" Chris ran ahead to catch up with her parents.

Shawn turned Rachel toward him and smiled. "That was a bribe."

Rachel shrugged. "Not really. It's hard on her to be left behind. I know I'd hate it."

"That's true. I will. This is it, Rachel," Shawn said as he squeezed her hand.

They'd reached the part of the terminal where only passengers were allowed. Mrs. Deering had already kissed her husband and daughter goodbye. She passed through the metal detectors and waited on the other side for Rachel.

"Bye, Dad. Bye, Chris." Rachel hugged them both.

"Knock 'em dead," her father whispered in her ear.

Then she turned and with her mother boarded the plane bound for New York. As Rachel strapped on her seat belt, she felt excited, but a little sad, too. In two weeks she'd be 14. And a student at the School of American Ballet in New York City.

And after her summer in New York, she had Shawn to come home to. That was the best of all! Life had a strange way of working out. And dreams had a funny way of coming true.

Author's Note

If you would like more information
about type 1 diabetes, please contact:

**Juvenile Diabetes
Research Foundation International**
120 Wall Street
New York, NY 10005-4001
Phone: 1-800-533-CURE (2873)
www.jdf.org

About the Author

LURLENE McDANIEL lives in Chattanooga, Tennessee, and is a favorite author of young people all over the country. Her best-selling books about kids overcoming problems such as cancer, diabetes, and the death of a parent or sibling draw a wide response from her readers. Lurlene says that the best compliment she can receive is having a reader tell her, "Your story was so interesting that I couldn't put it down!" To Lurlene, the most important thing is writing an uplifting story that helps the reader look at life from a different perspective.

Six Months to Live, the first of the four-book series about cancer survivor Dawn Rochelle, was placed in a time capsule at the Library of Congress in Washington, D.C. The capsule is scheduled to be opened in the year 2089.

Other Darby Creek Publishing books by Lurlene McDaniel include:

- *Six Months to Live*
- *I Want to Live*
- *No Time to Cry*
- *So Much to Live For*
- *Mother, Please Don't Die*
- *Why Did She Have to Die?*
- *If I Should Die Before I Wake*
- *My Secret Boyfriend*
- *A Horse for Mandy*